"Aren't we supposed to be practicing?"

Her eyes flew open, her cheeks hot with...something. Lust? Frustration? Frustrated lust? But before she could take him to task, she saw one corner of his mouth lift in amusement.

"Thought you liked it when I joked."

"All joking aside—" she cleared her throat "—there's no need to practice the physical part of this convenient marriage."

"You sure? A lengthy kiss usually follows the 'I dos.'"

"I'm pretty sure I can wing a chaste marital kiss. Even with you."

"You're the boss." His gaze drifted to her mouth, the move as sensual as if he'd leaned forward to press his lips to hers.

* * *

A Christmas Proposition
is part of the Dallas Billionaires Club series
from Jessica Lemmon!

Dear Reader,

What happens when two people who barely tolerate each other find themselves traveling and staying together and...planning their Christmas wedding? There are few tropes as fun as a marriage of convenience, and in *A Christmas Proposition*, sparks fly when Stefanie Ferguson, the youngest of the Ferguson siblings, finds herself proposing to her eldest brother's best friend and security detail.

Emmett Keaton has long protected the Ferguson family, but he's about to find out just how far he'll go to keep them safe—to keep *Stefanie* safe. He's the ultimate scrooge, and she loves Christmas, but he endures the holiday plans and mistletoe in favor of sharing a marital bed with her. Oh, and they wait until the deed is done to break the news of their nuptials to the rest of the family. As close as the Fergusons are, you can imagine how well that goes over.

Snuggle in and enjoy a story filled with tradition and fireworks between these two opposites. Stefanie and Emmett have a lot to learn about each other, and even more to learn about what it takes to be together forever and ever, amen. I have the utmost faith in them. If there's one attribute they both have in spades, it's stubbornness to see things through to the end. Once falling in love was added to the mix, they were goners.

Happy holidays,

Jessica Lemmon

www.JessicaLemmon.com

JESSICA LEMMON

———

A CHRISTMAS PROPOSITION

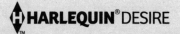

HARLEQUIN® DESIRE

Recycling programs
for this product may
not exist in your area.

ISBN-13: 978-1-335-97192-0

A Christmas Proposition

Copyright © 2018 by Jessica Lemmon

Printed in U.S.A.

A former job-hopper, **Jessica Lemmon** resides in Ohio with her husband and rescue dog. She holds a degree in graphic design currently gathering dust in an impressive frame. When she's not writing supersexy heroes, she can be found cooking, drawing, drinking coffee (okay, wine) and eating potato chips. She firmly believes God gifts us with talents for a purpose, and with His help, you can create the life you want.

Jessica is a social media junkie who loves to hear from readers. You can learn more at jessicalemmon.com.

Books by Jessica Lemmon

Harlequin Desire

Dallas Billionaires Club

Lone Star Lovers
A Snowbound Scandal
A Christmas Proposition

To Dad,
for always making Christmastime feel special
(PS: you can stop reading now).

One

December 20
Source: thedallasduchess.com
EXCLUSIVE:
STEFANIE FERGUSON AND BLAKE EASTWOOD
REUNION

Good morning, Dallas!

As maven of this fine city, the Dallas Duchess makes it her job to know the happenings of local royalty. In this town, no royalty is finer than the Fergusons.

"Princess" Stefanie Ferguson, socialite, heiress and party girl, has been spotted once again on the arm of cunning and charming Blake Eastwood, who just so happens to be the mayor's *biggest* opponent. (Naughty, naughty!) And, my savvy duchess dolls, you're all aware that the mayor=Stefanie's gorgeous and recently betrothed brother. Yes, ladies, another of Dallas's eligible bachelors is about to bite the dust.

(As an aside, you longtimers may recall my breaking story about the mayor shacking up in Montana during a snowstorm with his old flame. Hotcha! You always hear it here first.)

But back to Princess Stef and her dashing bad boy... By now you've no doubt seen the photo circulating on social media of Blake and Stefanie dancing cheek to cheek at a Toys for Tots fund-raiser. And if you're an astute observer like *moi*, you felt the sparks flying from that photo. As of right this very minute, I can confirm what my pitter-pattering heart was hoping for the most:

Stefanie and Blake are together!

Recently, I spoke with Blake and while I couldn't get him to commit to a timeline, I did learn a *verrrry* juicy bit of intel.

Dallas Duchess: I have to ask for the sake of my readers. Are you and Stefanie Ferguson seeing each other again?

Blake Eastwood: [emits a sexy chuckle] Um. Yes. We are.

DD: [squeals of delight] Can you tell me more?

BE: I can tell you that it's new, but serious.

DD: Put-a-ring-on-it serious?

BE: Come on, Duchess, I can't let every cat out of the bag.

DD: But it's almost Christmas! Surely you can give us one teeny-tiny hint?

BE: Christmastime is Stef's favorite time of the year. She whispered in my ear just yesterday that it's the perfect time to shop at Tiffany & Co. I'm a man who knows how to take a hint.

Ladies, gentlemen. If that's not a confirmation that Blake is popping the question Stefanie is *begging* him to ask, I don't know what is!

Go forth and share across social media with the links below. Looks like a Christmas engagement could be forthcoming!

Stefanie Ferguson paced the shining white floor of her sister-in-law's home office in a pair of knee-high, spike-heel Christian Louboutin boots. Unlike the last public relations hiccup she'd gotten into with Blake, this one couldn't be handled over a cup of coffee at Hip Stir.

Late last night, she'd been sipping on hot cocoa with Sambuca when she received a text from Blake.

Dallas Duchess has some news to share tomorrow. Me and you, gorgeous.

She'd pecked in an angry "Go to hell" followed by "Leave me alone" and then erased both lines in favor of ignoring him.

Lord only knew what he would've done with the screenshots if she'd texted him. It had taken everything in her not to respond to his baiting. Blake was Bad News with a capital *B* and *N*.

Last year, he'd gone to the Dallas Duchess via one

of her brother's staff members to break the story about Miriam Andrix returning to Chase's life. The write-up was in defense of Chase and almost lecturing Miriam for ruining the city's chaste mayor. Ridiculous. It was clear to anyone who saw them together that Miriam and Chase were gaga over each other—even Stefanie could see that, and she was Chase's sister.

Blake's original motivation for his nefarious smear campaign was building a new civic center, which he wanted to erect *very close* to Ferguson Oil property. Chase had been saying no for years. Blake had promised to "ruin him" if it was the last thing he did, as if he were some sort of mustache-twisting bandit.

Stef reminded herself, again, that she hadn't known the dirty details when Blake charmed her into his hotel bed one lonely night a few years back. She certainly had never expected him to release pictures of them leaving the hotel together.

Penelope Ferguson had summoned a PR magic spell to bail Stef out of her Blake-related problem then, and she'd had a hand in smoothing over Chase and Miriam's relationship last year. With Chase's imminent reelection looming—Stef refused to consider the possibility of him losing—she had zero worries that Pen would be able to work her magic again and smooth this one over, as well.

"You should've called me the second Blake the Snake sent you that text," Penelope scolded from where she sat in front of her computer screen. Her full mouth was a firm line of displeasure, her eyes narrowed in frustration.

Stef stopped pacing and wrapped herself protectively in her own arms. "It was late. I didn't want to bother you."

And she hadn't wanted her sister-in-law to hear the

raw vulnerability in her voice. Stef might have refused to respond with the intent of letting Blake know how little he'd affected her, but in truth he had. Like the first time those hotel photos saw the light of day, she felt cheap and used.

He'd been charming and—she'd thought—vulnerable the night he'd told her he wanted her. She'd been fresh off a breakup and vulnerable herself. A night with an attractive man who appreciated her—even one who disagreed with her brother the mayor—was supposed to have boosted her confidence and relieved a long drought of physical affection.

They'd both been attending a boring fund-raiser at the time. Champagne had flowed and he'd been accommodating and, she knew now, lying. He'd been seeking revenge on Chase and would take any of the Fergusons as his pound of flesh. She'd allowed herself to be talked into going to bed with him and she still felt the sting of embarrassment and anger at her naïveté.

The next day, the photos had surfaced and she'd been accused of slutting around with the mayor's nemesis.

And now this.

"When was the fund-raiser where this was taken?" Pen turned her laptop screen to show the most recent leaked photo of Blake and Stef cheek to cheek on the dance floor.

"Last weekend."

"You're looking cozy."

"He asked me to dance by taking my hand and dragging me to the floor. I didn't want to cause a scene by telling him where to shove his invitation."

She'd caused enough problems for her brother and his campaign. Chase didn't hold her accountable, but she couldn't unshoulder her fair share of responsibility.

"What you don't see in this photo is that I'm telling him off. I used some very unladylike language, hence my leaning in close. I told him if he didn't leave me and my family alone, I'd castrate him with a pair of dull shears."

Stef smiled, proud. At least she'd stood up for herself then. Pen wasn't smiling with her.

"What you did was step into a snare of his making, Stefanie. *Again*." Pen shook her head. "He timed the release of this photo on purpose, to coincide with the reelection. Why is he hinting that you two are going to be married?"

Stef felt her cheeks warm as she recalled the rest of her conversation that night. "That…is partially my fault."

Pen raised her eyebrows and waited.

Stef, you'll be single forever with a mouth like that. You have to be a good little girl if you ever hope to land a husband. Blake had swept her in another circle on the dance floor while her ire had risen to dangerous levels.

Ha! You're one to talk. Is there a female on this planet who would willingly perch in your family tree or do you have to trick them all into going to bed with you?

You came willingly. A few times if memory serves.

"He was holding me tight, and twisting away didn't loosen his hold on my waist." Stef licked her lips, regretting her words now that she'd felt the sting of retaliation. "I may have mentioned something about a 'tiny prick' and 'faking it' and that if he didn't let me go, I'd tell everyone within earshot how unsatisfying it was to be bedded by Blake the Snake."

Pen's eyebrows climbed higher on her forehead, and just when Stef was sure she'd be read the riot act, her sister-in-law's smile burst forth like the sun after a hard rain.

"You know how to find trouble, don't you?" Pen asked through a laugh. She must've caught Stef's crestfallen features when she looked up because she was out of her chair in a shot. "I'm sorry I said that. Ignore me."

Pen grabbed Stef's shoulders and Stef felt the wobble in her chin paired with heat behind her eyes.

"I don't try to."

"I didn't mean it that way. Seriously." Pen pulled Stef into a hug.

Stef felt like a fragile piece of china lately, not wanting to be in the way of Chase's campaign or too involved while Pen and Zach raised their daughter. Heck, even Mom and Dad were going through a second honeymoon phase, so Stef was trying to stay out from underfoot in that capacity, as well.

"You can fix this." Stef swallowed her budding tears. "You have unraveled some of the biggest knots in Dallas since you moved here. Tell me the easiest, fastest, most succinct way to crush this fake news."

"As a woman who had her own false engagement to contend with—" Pen smirked "—I *have* had experience with this sort of thing. Only the 'groom' was your brother and part of the plan."

"And Blake's a renegade douchebag."

Of all the bad decisions Stef had made during her thirty brief years on this planet, why this one? Why had she fallen victim to that man's false charms?

"If you were anyone other than my sister-in-law, I'd advise you to get married."

"To Blake?" Stef practically shrieked.

"No! My God. *No.* I'm saying the best way to trump

Blake's claim that he's engaged to you is to marry someone else. Know any eligible bachelors?"

Stef was staring in shock. This certainly wasn't the advice she'd expected to get from Penelope.

"I'm *joking*." Pen gave Stef's shoulders a little shake before moving back to her desk. Laptop open, she started typing. "I'll craft a plan to detangle this mess that will work for you and your brother the mayor."

"Thank you."

Pen smiled up at her. "And I promise it *won't* involve nuptials."

Two

Emmett Keaton had been Chase Ferguson's close friend, arguably his best friend, since college.

He could say with authority that Chase rarely allowed his feathers to ruffle. But today his feathers weren't only ruffled, they were scattered to the four corners of the earth.

Since it was Emmett's job to keep the mayor's office safe, he'd have to assume the role of "the calm one" today. As the scandal currently wreaking havoc had to do with Stefanie, he found it challenging to bank his own anger.

The youngest Ferguson had a talent for finding trouble.

"When I get my hands on that sniveling weasel," Chase grated out through teeth that were welded together, "I swear on everything holy—"

"Chase." Penelope—wife to Chase's brother, Zach—

stood in front of Chase's desk, arms crossed. She was dressed in a white pantsuit, her long blond hair pulled into a neat twist at the back of her head. Her stance broadcast one undeniable truth: she wasn't intimidated by power. She'd handled many a powerful man as a public relations specialist over the years, and had become a trusted friend when Chase hired her to care for Stef the first time she stepped in it with Blake fucking Eastwood.

Because Chase trusted her, Emmett did, also.

"I've got this," Pen said. "You have nothing to worry about."

A muscle in Chase's jaw ticked but he gave his sister-in-law a curt nod. She returned it with one of her own and spun on one very high-heeled shoe to leave.

Once she was out the door, Chase glanced at Emmett with irises so dark they bordered on black.

Chase punched a button on his phone. "Cynthia. Get my sister on the line."

"Yes, sir."

"Sure you want to do that, boss?" Emmett asked.

Chase didn't answer.

A moment later, the desk phone rang.

"Where the hell are you?" Chase barked into the receiver. A brief pause and then, "You have thirty seconds." He slammed the phone down on its base and glared at the only target in the room. Emmett took the blow without flinching. "She was already on her way."

"Good."

Chase needed to redirect his anger? *Fine.*

It was better than him unleashing it on Stefanie.

The door burst open almost exactly thirty seconds later. Stefanie strode into the office in a short red designer dress, tall boots with dangerous-looking heels and a painted pout in siren red.

"I saw Pen on my way in." Stef tucked her cell phone into an oversize handbag. "She warned me that you weren't in the best mood. I'm assuming you're mad at me."

Nostrils flared, Chase pulled in a deep breath through his nose. When he spoke, his words were carefully measured. "I'm not angry with you, Stefanie. I'm—"

"Don't say *disappointed*." She dropped the handbag onto the leather chair in the corner of the room and sent Emmett a derisive glare.

Typical.

She hated him for reasons he'd yet to discern. He'd only ever offered assistance when she'd needed him— whether she'd asked or not. If memory served, she'd never asked.

"I'm *concerned*," Chase said, and her head swiveled back to her brother. "Your Christmas retreat is soon, yes?"

"Yes." A smile of pure delight crested her red mouth.

That smile lit her face like a string of holiday lights. Emmett had never seen someone so in love with the idea of Christmas. Loving the holiday was as foreign to him as understanding anything else about the lush lifestyle his best friend's family led. In spite of his own amassed fortune, Emmett had no desire for frills of any kind. And he certainly had no desire to celebrate an occasion that brought forth bad memories and worse consequences.

"Where is it this year?" Chase asked.

"San Antonio."

"Cancel it."

Her face morphed into tortured shock. "What? Never. Absolutely not."

"That wasn't a request. There was no question mark at the end of my sentence." Chase pointed at her, his quaking arm revealing his anger. "Because you don't have the sense to stay away from Blake Eastwood, my campaign is suffering from the fallout."

Emmett's hands balled into fists at his sides.

He was rarely in disagreement with his friend, but in this case, Chase's comments were out of line. Stef had been briefly involved with Blake—whom Emmett would love to go a round or two with, bare-knuckle—but the accusation that she was to blame was harsh.

"Whatever you have to do in San Antonio with your girlfriends can be done from Dallas just as easily. You're not leaving the city, and if you do go out, you're going to be chaperoned. Do you understand me?"

Her stricken expression faded into a laugh of disbelief. "You can't ground me, Chase. You're not my father. And even if you were Dad, he can't ground me, either. I'm thirty years old!"

"Then why are you acting like a spoiled teenager?" Chase roared.

"Hey!" Emmett's outburst was so unexpected that both Fergusons faced him wearing shell-shocked expressions.

He took a step closer to Chase, instinct more than decision driving him. "Let's keep the blame where it should be. *On Blake.* Stefanie's been through enough. She doesn't need you piling on."

Chase's lips pressed into a thin, frustrated frown. Then he pinched the bridge of his nose, took a deep breath and leaned both hands flat on his desk.

Emmett flickered a glance over at Stefanie, who, for

the first time in her life, regarded him with something akin to gratitude. He wasn't sure what to do with that.

"I'm asking, Stefanie—" Chase addressed his blotter before sitting in his chair and meeting his sister's eyes "—for your cooperation."

"Penelope is amazing at her job. There's no reason she can't—"

"I'm *asking*," Chase repeated, his voice firmer.

"I look forward to this retreat every year. I can't cancel an event that happens in four days."

"Why not?" Chase's forehead dented. "Can't you and your girlfriends drink champagne and talk about fashion another time? Mail them their gifts. Hell, invite them here. You can host at my mansion."

"I...can't do that." She regarded her impractical boots, appearing tormented by the idea of canceling.

Disappointment, Emmett could understand. Torment didn't make a hell of a lot of sense.

Stef loved her family above all else. Over the years, Emmett had witnessed the special bond she and Chase had—she respected her brother. And she would never lie to him. So why was Emmett getting the distinct impression that she was trying hard not to do just that? Why couldn't she party here in town? Why did she have to travel to San Antonio?

She wasn't lying—not yet—but she was definitely keeping from saying too much.

"Plans can be changed. I'll foot the bill for it, if you like," Chase told her. "I'll grease some palms and find you a last-minute venue in Dallas. You can't leave town with this mark on your back. I forbid it."

"What mark? Do you think I'm going to be kidnapped by Blake's henchmen or something?" Stef let out an exasperated laugh. Emmett didn't find it funny.

His back went ramrod straight, his senses on high alert at the idea that any harm would befall her.

He forbade it.

"You do things without thinking," the mayor said. "Who knows what could happen?"

"Chase, that's enough." Emmett took a step closer—to Stefanie this time.

His friend was right to watch out for his youngest sibling, but he was handling this wrong. Not that Emmett had much experience with sensitivity—he had been raised by Van Keaton, after all. But Emmett knew Stef and he also knew the situation. He couldn't keep from stepping at least one toe in her corner.

"You can stand down," Stef snapped. "I don't need your protection from my stupid brother."

"You need protection from yourself," Chase interjected.

This conversation was getting nowhere.

"I'm going to San Antonio tomorrow," she said. "I'll be back in a few days. I'm sure your *precious* campaign will be intact when I return." She grabbed her handbag and slung it over her shoulder as Chase rose from his chair, his face a beet-worthy shade of red.

"I'll drive you," Emmett blurted.

Again he was faced by both Fergusons. But only one of them looked upset by his offer. The cute blonde one.

"Yes. Great idea." Chase nodded. "Emmett will be your escort."

"I don't want an escort!"

"I don't care!"

"Knock it off." Emmett bodily moved himself to stand between Stefanie and Chase. "I'll drive you to San Antonio. Book me a room wherever you're staying."

"It's a bed-and-breakfast and it's *full*." She raised her chin, her aquamarine eyes flashing in warning.

"I'll sleep in my SUV." Emmett tipped his head in challenge. "It's either this or you don't go. Your brother's right about it being dangerous. Your image is plastered all over social media. I've seen you in the spotlight before. Paparazzi chase you, Stef."

She was beautiful and young and easily the most famous female billionaire in Dallas, if not the state of Texas. The combination of her it-girl reputation and a rumor that she was going to marry the mayor's sworn enemy made for tempting media fodder.

She opened her mouth, probably to argue.

Emmett lifted his eyebrows, silently communicating. *Give me a break, okay?*

Miraculously, rather than arguing, she gritted out, "Fine."

"Great. Get out," Chase said. "Both of you."

So, his best friend was prickly. So what? Emmett wasn't one for being handled with kid gloves. His rhino-tough hide had been hewed at a young age.

"Come on," he told Stef, opening the mayor's door for her to exit. "I'll give you a ride home."

Emmett held open the passenger door of his black SUV, a gas-guzzling, tinted-windowed, way-too-big-for-a-road-trip vehicle.

"You can't be serious about taking this beast to San Antonio. We'll have to pull over every fifteen miles to refill the tank."

"Get. In."

She glared up at his chiseled jaw and perfectly shaped head beneath very short, dark brown hair. He wore it cropped close and rarely was it more than a few inches long on top. He was bedecked in what she'd come to think of as his "standard uniform." A crisp white shirt open at the collar and dark slacks. His brawn and bulk and attitude were better suited for a T-shirt and sweats, but his job title required a dab of formality.

She tossed her purse inside and grasped the SUV's door handle and the front seat to climb in. Emmett's warm, broad palm cupped her elbow to steady her, and she nearly jerked away in shock. If she wasn't mistaken, that was the first time he'd ever touched her.

It was…alarming.

And not in the get-your-damn-hands-off-me kind of way. His touch had felt…*intimate*.

Once she was inside he dropped his voice and leaned close. She ignored the clean leather smell of him. Or tried to, anyway.

"Heads up. There's a suspicious cyclist over there." He shut her door and walked around to the driver's side.

She scanned the immediate area outside her brother's office twice before she spotted a casual-looking guy on a bike with a cell phone conspicuously propped on the handlebars and pointing at the SUV.

Damn.

As much as she hated to admit it, Chase might have had a point about media attention.

Emmett settled into the driver's seat and turned over the engine, sending her an assessing, stony gray stare. Typically, his eyes held a note of blue, but today they mirrored the cloudy skies above.

"What?" she barked. "Do you want me to congratulate you because you're right?"

He smirked. "Buckle your belt."

"Let's get one thing straight, Neanderthal," she said

as she jerked the belt over her torso. "You may believe a woman's place is in the passenger seat. Or that I can't handle anything on my own without one of you *big strong* men to help me out, but FYI, I am not yours to command."

Though some foreign tingly part of her suggested that Emmett might be the perfect specimen to take commands *from*.

She swallowed the rest of her speech about being an adult and handling her own problems, mainly because they both felt like stretches of the truth. In all of her attempts not to involve her family in her life, she'd somehow managed to tow them in. Her parents, Chase, Penelope, Zach and now Emmett.

Angry with herself more than her driver, she stared out the window in silence as the SUV pulled away from the curb.

Three

Stef had gone to bed late last night, staring at the ceiling for a long while, her mind lost on her current predicament.

She hadn't stayed up late to pack—she'd done that already and her matching luggage was lined up dutifully next to her apartment door. Knowing that Emmett would pick her up promptly at 7:00 a.m., she also hadn't indulged in more than one glass of sparkling rosé before bed. No, her insomnia couldn't be blamed on a lack of planning or too much alcohol. She'd lain awake, earning this morning's puffy eyes and groggy brain for one reason.

She was tired of being everyone else's problem.

It wasn't enough to tell her parents and her brothers that she was an adult. She had to *show* them. In order to show them, she needed to take care of the Blake situation herself.

Penelope was equipped to handle any PR disaster, but the more Stef thought about it, the more Pen's plan to "wait and see" sounded like a slow track to a solution. Chase's election was less than six months away. Stefanie refused to let Blake continue to drag her family's good name through the muck.

Chase had made it clear last fall that he didn't hold Stefanie accountable for her act of indiscretion with Blake. In spite of his absolving her, her guilt remained.

That Blake held this much power over her infuriated her. She refused to let him cause her to lose even one more minute of sleep.

Last night while staring at the ceiling of her apartment, she'd decided not to let Blake have that power over her family, either.

Penelope's words rang in her ears.

If you were anyone other than my sister-in-law, I'd advise you to get married.

Well, why hadn't that been Pen's suggestion? It shouldn't matter that Stefanie was her sister-in-law. A solution was a solution! There was only one *eensy-weensy* problem. Stefanie would have to find someone to marry, and fast.

She wasn't sure who to approach, let alone how to ask. She'd climbed out of bed during the wee hours, unhooked her phone from the charger in her kitchen and poured one more small glass of wine. Then she started scrolling through her contacts in her phone's address book.

Every prospect she thumbed through seemed worse than the last. She passed over ex-boyfriends, hookups and acquaintances alike. None of them were marriage material—not even temporarily. Plus, how would she ask for a favor like that from someone she hadn't talked to in months, or years in some cases?

Hi, I know you haven't heard from me for a while, but would you mind marrying me for a few months?

Not to mention she would need her groom to keep their marriage arrangement a secret. The entire purpose of the ruse would be to convince the press and that horrible blogger woman that Stefanie wasn't involved with Blake. Then Blake would be forced to recant his bullshit statement.

After she'd thought it through, she decided an engagement announcement would look like a desperate cover-up. It gave Blake too much wiggle room, and she couldn't risk him slithering into her family's life again.

Wineglass empty and fatigue finally overcoming her, Stef had dragged herself to the couch, pulled a blanket over her body and caught about three hours of tossing-turning sleep.

The knock on her front door came way too early, even though she was ready for it. She'd pulled her hair into a sloppy bun on top of her head, dashed on a layer of makeup and donned big, dark sunglasses so that *if* a photo was snapped of her in the wild, she wouldn't look like she'd had a sleepless night fretting over Blake.

Stef had called Pen yesterday afternoon and suggested releasing a statement that she was no more marrying Blake than she was marrying Kermit the Frog, but Pen had recommended against it.

We can't turn this into he said, she said, especially while you're out of town. Let's let the dust settle and we'll handle things in the new year. Enjoy your Christmas party!

Despite what she'd led everyone to believe, Stef wasn't going to a Christmas party with her girlfriends.

She was hosting a massive charity dinner that she'd arranged for some of the poorest families in Harlington, a city outside San Antonio.

Over the last three Christmas Eves, she'd hosted similar dinners and, so far, had kept her little Christmas secret. She didn't want publicity or attention for it—not yet. She wanted to do it her way, and *without* input from family members on how to arrange the place settings or what kind of food to serve.

Providing for the less fortunate and giving back filled her with a sense of satisfaction like nothing else. To Stef, this dinner party was about more than writing a check. She'd personally witnessed gratitude and happiness on the faces of men, women and children who otherwise wouldn't have had a merry Christmas.

Hiding what she was doing from her family wasn't too difficult, but keeping her identity a secret from her guests was a bit trickier. So far so good—no one had recognized her yet. She might be widely recognized by the snooty Dallas upper crust, but to the hardworking people of Texas proper, she was simply a young woman helping out.

Her goal was to grow the charity event larger starting next year, which would mean she'd need to reveal her true identity in order to expand and give it the attention it deserved. But she couldn't do that while living in the Ferguson shadow or tiptoeing around her brother and his career as mayor.

Yes, going public would mean she'd have to do a bit of pruning to her own reputation before next Christmas.

"Coming!" she called when the knock at the door came again.

She rushed to the door and held it open, but rather

than ushering Emmett forward, she ended up walking outside into the cold with him.

"Is that snow? Oh my gosh, that's snow!"

Snow in Texas was a rare occasion. Typically this time of year temperatures hovered in the forties.

"Yeah—hey, where are you going?"

She ignored him to step out onto her upstairs front stoop. The snow wasn't sticking, sadly, but the flakes were enough to fill her heart with joy. Each delicate, sparkly and, yes, *sloppy* flake was a reminder that her favorite holiday was nearly upon them.

"It's beautiful."

"It's wet. Inconvenient. And not why I live in Texas."

She frowned at Emmett. In a black leather coat, his white collared shirt visible just beneath the open zipper, and his standard black pants and leather boots, he should look like a tall, attractive, sturdy man she could count on. Instead, he was a grousing, grumpy individual set on ruining her good mood.

"It's *magical*. And I refuse to let you make me feel bad about that."

She slapped a palm against his broad chest, shoving him aside. Okay, so she didn't so much shove him as push against a chest made of solid muscle that had no give whatsoever. No matter! Emmett Keaton was not going to ruin her day. She'd already given that power away, and all too recently. It was a mistake she vowed not to repeat.

"I'll just take these *magical* bags out to my *mystical* SUV and wait for you to float on down, then," he said as he picked up her luggage.

Humming a Christmas tune to drown out Scrooge Keaton, she snagged her coffee thermos out from under the single-cup coffee maker and snapped on the lid. She might have to spend several days with him, but thank God the car ride was only four hours long.

How much damage could he do in four hours?

Hour One

"No Christmas music."

"That's inhumane."

She stabbed the button on the radio to turn it on and Emmett pushed a button on the steering wheel to shut it off.

"Can you explain to me how I am on my way to a Christmas celebration—that you have volunteered to drive me to, by the way—and yet I'm not allowed to listen to Christmas music on the drive over?"

"My car. My rules."

"That was rhetorical. Don't be a grump." She turned on the music again, and again Emmett turned it off. "What if the volume is really, really low?"

He didn't pull his eyes from the road, not even to glare at her.

"Fine. I'll talk instead." She cleared her throat. "So, I found this dress for my mother's art show next month. It's blue and sparkly and goes perfectly with my new shoes that I bought from—"

A long-suffering sigh sounded from his chest, and Emmett powered on the radio in surrender. He thumbed down the volume button on the steering wheel, but she considered it a win.

Hour Two

"I don't see why we couldn't stop at a decent restaurant and order takeout." She held the fast-food bag between a finger and thumb and eyed the grease spots that had seeped through the paper dubiously. "There are approximately a million calories in this bag. If I'm going to consume a million calories, it'd better be a gourmet meal."

Emmett stuck his hand into the bag and came out with one of the cheeseburgers. She watched as he unwrapped the sandwich, took a huge bite and, because that move took both hands, drove with his knee.

Because he was big enough to drive with his knee.

One booted foot firmly on the floor, his left knee kept the SUV perfectly positioned in the center of the lane.

What an irritatingly sexy move that was. Why did he have to be so damn capable at everything?

She rummaged through the bag until she found her sandwich. A fish sandwich had been the least calorie-laden item on the menu. It was roughly the size of a silver dollar, smashed flat, and half the cheese was glued to the cardboard container rather than on the bun.

"Great."

Emmett's hand plunged into the bag again and he came out with a container of fries. The burger held in one hand, he wedged the fry container between his big thighs and shoved three or four fries into his mouth. Even with one cheek stuffed like a chipmunk's, he didn't appear any less capable.

She'd been around strong men all her life. Her father and her brothers were all strong, commanding, decisive men.

Emmett had those traits as well, but it came in a less refined package. Sure, he dressed well, but there was a rough-hewn edge beneath that Armani shirt.

It bothered her. It bothered her because it didn't make any sense.

It bothers you because you find it attractive.

Just like she'd found Blake attractive? Just like she'd found plenty of other men who were all wrong for her attractive?

She nibbled on the edge of her fish sandwich, sending a longing look to the fries nestled between Emmett's legs.

"See something you like?" He crumpled the empty burger wrapper and tossed it into the fast-food bag at her feet.

She jerked her gaze to his face and was alarmed to find him smiling over at her.

"No. I don't," she argued a little too fervently.

His smile remained. Eyes on the road, he proffered the container of fries.

Rather than resist, she plucked out three perfectly golden, salty potatoes and reminded herself that the bossy, attractive man in the driver's seat was as bad for her as this meal.

Four

Hour Three

Emmett slid a look over at Stefanie, who was intently scrolling through her phone and had been for the last several miles. What the hell was she doing?

"You're going to make yourself carsick," he grumbled.

He could feel her eyes on him. Wide, innocent eyes.

He didn't understand that observation about her, but it was nonetheless true. The only Ferguson daughter wasn't naive or immature. She was headstrong and mulish, and he knew from experience, since he had both those attributes in spades. When they belonged to a woman, however, people saw her as a trite, vapid troublemaker.

Frankly, it pissed him off. He'd known Stef for as long as he'd known Chase, and she wasn't any of those things. But she must've been immune to what the public said about her. She never complained about her image or tried to make herself smaller because the media talked about her.

"You do your thing, I'll do mine." Her snide remark made him smile in spite of himself.

His "thing" at the moment was chauffeuring her safely from Dallas to San Antonio so that she could hobnob with her friends and ignore him. Which was what being around her was always like. He'd been joking about sleeping in the SUV, but he assumed he could find a last-minute room. San Antonio was a big city.

He checked the rearview mirror and noticed the same black sedan he'd clocked earlier. It trailed three or four cars behind him. He wasn't so paranoid that he believed they were being followed—it was a highway and they were all heading the same direction—but neither would he take Stef's safety for granted.

He'd been in the habit of looking out for her over the past couple of years, so he supposed that was the reason he'd offered himself up as the human sacrifice rather than asking her to change her plans.

First off, he knew she wouldn't. And if she'd gone anyway, he'd have been the one tailing her right now.

Another glance showed the black sedan sliding into the same lane and vanishing behind a semi.

It was early yet. He'd keep an eye on it.

Both eyes.

Hour Four

Stef paused her scrolling through her address book, which she'd been desperately searching for a man to marry her for show.

She was young, rich and attractive, yet this was proving to be an insurmountable task. Every name she passed on the list was either seeing someone or the wrong choice. Like Oliver James, for example.

She and Oliver had casually dated for three months last summer. He was a successful commercial real estate buyer and a few years older than her. They'd stopped seeing each other mutually when things had simmered down.

She'd been contemplating texting him to find out if he was still single when Emmett spoke up to ask her if she was cold and snapped her out of her imaginings. Just as well. Oliver was a nice enough guy, but she didn't know if she could trust him when it came to being discreet. He was showy with a big personality. Always telling a joke or commanding the attention of the room.

Definitely not a good choice for an undercover marriage.

Now, though, her eyes rested on a name that she hadn't considered before. She blinked, considered what she knew of the man and wondered if she could slot him into the role of groom even on a pretend-temporary basis.

Emmett Keaton.

She wrinkled her nose, but the distaste she tried to feel wasn't there.

Stefanie Keaton.

It might work.

At first blush, the idea seemed insane, but when she allowed herself to walk through the steps of arranging a wedding to the man driving, it wasn't so insane.

Emmett didn't like her and she didn't like him that

much, either. Ending a marriage when it was time
would be as natural as breathing for them.

She looked up "marriage licenses in Harlington" on
her phone and Google provided the website for the city.
She hadn't exactly lied about going to San Antonio. The
smaller district was located about thirty minutes outside
San Antonio. If she had told Chase that she was heading
to the one-horse town to visit her high-class friends, he
would've known something was up.

She hadn't told Emmett yet, but they weren't close
to where he needed to pull off the highway. She opened
a map. In about twenty miles, he'd need to reroute.

Back to the issue at hand: marrying Emmett.

The marriage license had a seventy-two-hour waiting period. If they applied today… She counted the days
on her fingers. They'd be good to go by Christmas Eve.
The question was, could she find someone to marry
them at the last minute on a holiday?

She opened her email app and pecked out a corre-
spondence to the woman who ran the B and B where
Stef had made her reservations.

Hi, Margaret,
Do you know anyone who could marry a couple on
Christmas Eve?

She watched out the windshield, considering the
timing of the charity dinner. It was a six o'clock dinner, and even with cleanup she'd be out of there by ten
o'clock. Once they returned to the B and B, changed
into whatever wedding attire she was able to scrounge
up in the three-day gap between license and "I do,"
that'd mean…

Preferably midnight, she typed. As Christmas Eve turns to Christmas day.

She smiled to herself as she finished the email. Married at midnight on Christmas day. Could it be more perfect?

She slanted a glance at Emmett and frowned. Maybe *perfect* was overshooting it. She hoped he could summon up an expression other than "The Grinch Who Stole Christmas" for a few of the photos.

She should probably make sure Emmett didn't have a secret wife or girlfriend first. He kept his personal life in Stef's blind spot. She knew him in relation only to what he did at the mayor's office, and even then it looked to her like a bunch of walking around while wearing a starched white button-down shirt and a stern expression.

"Do you date?"

Emmett snapped his head around, a look of incredulity on his face. "What?"

"Date. Do you date?"

If she wasn't mistaken, he squirmed in his seat.

"Women. Men. Anyone?"

"Women." His frown intensified.

"Are you dating anyone right now?"

He said nothing, both hands on the wheel in an elbows-locked position.

"Why?" he finally muttered.

It seemed too early to blurt out that she wanted to marry him. She'd have to ease into that request.

"Just making conversation. I never see you with anyone whenever you're at a family function."

"That's work."

"You can't work all the time."

"I can. I do."

Yeah, this was getting her nowhere.

"Your head is the perfect shape. Not everyone can wear their hair that short."

"The deep car chatter continues."

"I'm just saying, I'm sure you can find a date even though your personality is basically the worst."

His shoulders jumped in what might have been a laugh, but no smile yet.

She smiled, enjoying a challenge. "So? Do you date?"

"Not as much as you do."

She ignored the jab. "Are you seeing anyone right now?"

"Yes. You. *Exclusively.*"

He didn't take his eyes off the road to look at her so he didn't see her bite her lip in consideration. As segues went, this was pretty much her only chance.

"I talked to Penelope about how to handle the Blake situation. Know what she said?"

"Stay out of it and let her do her job?"

Almost verbatim, but that wasn't what Stef was getting at.

"She said that if I were anyone else, she'd suggest I get married."

"She would suggest you pretend you're married?" he asked, his tone flat.

"No. She would suggest I literally get married. Marriage licenses are public record. Any reporter worth her salt could verify if it was real or not."

Emmett said nothing.

"I've been scrolling through my phone in search of Mr. Stefanie Ferguson, but no luck. I'm almost halfway through the alphabet."

He changed lanes, the mar in his brow deepening.

"You're going to have a lot of wrinkles when you're old because of the frowning. Did you know that—"

"It takes more muscles to frown than smile? Yes. I knew that."

"Anyway, when I find my husband-to-be, it'll only have to last until the election. Once Chase is reelected as mayor, I can annul it, no harm no foul."

A minute of silence passed, the only sound in the car a Mariah Carey holiday tune playing quietly on the radio. Emmett stabbed a button on the steering wheel to shut it off.

"You have to take this exit for where we're going."

"I don't think so."

"I know so." She held her phone up and showed him the map.

"Where is that?" he asked, even as he dutifully changed lanes.

"I lied about San Antonio. We're going to a town called Harlington. It's just outside—"

"I know Harlington." His visage darkened.

"You do?" She'd assumed he was from a similarly wealthy Dallas background as her family. At least upper middle class. "Here. This exit." She rested her cell phone on the dash, and though he mumbled a swear word under his breath, he pulled off the exit.

"From here take route—"

"I can read the map, Stefanie."

Yeah, proposing should work out great, she thought with an eye roll.

She waited a few more silent minutes before turning on the radio again. The Sting song didn't cause her driver to visibly wince.

Her email notification lit up her phone and she

opened her inbox to read Margaret's reply, whose answer was an exuberant "Yes!"

Evidently Margaret's son was a minister and available on Christmas Eve for a midnight wedding. In the next paragraph of her reply, Margaret went on and on about the beautiful decorations in the sitting room of her old Victorian house.

Stefanie responded with a quick message. I'm working out the marriage license now.

Little did Emmett know, the address she'd keyed into her map was for city hall downtown.

Five

"Which building?" Emmett drove through the thick traffic of downtown Harlington.

Yeah, he knew this town. He'd grown up not far from here. Before he'd escaped to go to college. Before happenstance had put him at the same wild frat party as Chase Ferguson. They'd stopped in the center of the room en route to flirt with the same girl. Neither of them had won the girl, but they'd forged a strong friendship.

From there, Emmett's world had forked. He'd left behind his former life as a rough kid from a lonely home. He'd dropped out of college and never finished, but his old man hadn't noticed. Van Keaton had been lost in his own prison of grief since the Christmas that'd robbed both him and Emmett of all that was good.

Since then, Emmett had been determined to create good. In addition to working with Chase as his head of security, Emmett had also learned how to invest well. Hell, he'd mimicked his friend's financial habits, had read every book Chase recommended and had listened to countless podcasts on the topic. It never would've occurred to Emmett that he could live the way he lived now if it wasn't for the Fergusons. They took the idea of "living well" to an advanced level.

Emmett's work at the mayor's office might as well be his source of oxygen. He had the Fergusons, who had been a placeholder for the family Emmett rarely saw. His father was a lonely man determined to bask in his own misery, so Emmett let him do it. And he'd never gone home on a holiday. Van didn't do holidays. Not anymore.

And neither did Emmett.

Stef squealed from the passenger seat, going on about how "beautiful" the red bows and pine boughs tied to paint-chipped lampposts were, but he could only offer a grunt.

Those tattered pine boughs had seen better days and the red ribbons drooped. The shop windows downtown covered in spray snow would require tedious scraping with a razor blade to come clean, and the strings of white lights wrapped around every lamppost served as a reminder of what once was but could never be again.

"Where the hell is this place?" he asked at a stoplight. He didn't see any building resembling a B and B.

"Oh. Um. I have to stop at city hall first."

She directed him to the tall brick building between a shoe shop and a store called the Fan Man, which, as far as Emmett could tell, sold ceiling fans and lighting fixtures.

"What for?" He navigated to an open parking spot,

but when she took off her seat belt, he caught the strip of nylon in one fist. She sagged back into her seat.

"I know you think the idea of me marrying someone sounds—"

"Insane," he finished for her, letting her go.

"Think about it, Em. Blake won't have a leg to stand on. I refuse to let him use a mistake I made in the past against my family."

Every time he pictured her with that guy, rage spilled into his bloodstream.

"It was the worst mistake of my life."

"Huge," he grumbled in agreement.

Guilt outlined her pretty features.

It was the wrong thing for him to say. Blake was predatory and single-minded. And when Chase had found out his sister slept with that pig, his reaction had mirrored Emmett's. Emmett would've happily castrated the bastard to ensure he'd never hurt anyone again.

"There are worse things in life," he told Stef. "Trust me."

Christmas shoppers flooded the streets, bustling around to finish their shopping before it was too late, many with small children in tow. One little boy with dark hair and pink cheeks rode in a stroller and pointed with one mitten as snow began to fall, and Emmett's heart crushed.

That kid was the same age as his brother, Michael, when he'd passed.

"I was awake for hours last night trying to think of a suitable groom, but after a quick scan of my contacts I came up empty-handed. I decided to check again today in case I'd overlooked someone and then I found my-self lingering over a name…"

"Completely insane." He shook his head.

"Do you know why?"

He did look at her now, having neither any idea why nor any clue as to how she thought this was the best way to proceed.

"Because I came across the only name in my address book that belonged to someone who cares enough about my brother to agree to my plan."

Something tender invaded her expression. He'd never until this moment been regarded by Stefanie Ferguson with "tenderness."

Hell if he knew what to do with that.

"You." She said the word with finality.

"Me what?" he asked, the question loud in the cab of the SUV.

"You are the only man who would be discreet, go along with my plan and, provided you don't already have a girlfriend, fiancée or wife—"

"You think I have a wife?" There was a crazy idea. Even crazier was the idea that Stefanie would *be* that wife. He reached for his cup of gas station coffee, wincing when the mouthful was cold instead of hot.

"There's a seventy-two-hour waiting period, so we have to apply for the license today. Then we can be married on Christmas Eve after my…um… After I visit my friends."

"Forget it." He put the SUV in Reverse to wiggle from the parking space when her hand—and cold, delicate fingers—brushed his.

Her touch was foreign, as most touches were to him, yet familiar in a way he couldn't understand. Maybe because he'd known her for so long. Other than her mother, Eleanor Ferguson, Stefanie had been the only constant woman in his life since he was a very small boy.

"I've worked out everything. All you have to do is agree and smile for the camera so I can leak a few photos to social media. That's it. Two little things."

"Little?" His incredulous laugh cracked the air. "You're suggesting we get *married*, Stef. There's nothing little about that ask."

"The end game is to screw over Blake and save Chase's campaign. It's noble. You'd be doing your civic duty."

"There's got to be another way."

It was nuts. He couldn't consider this.

So why was he?

"Well. I guess I could pay someone to marry me."

"Absolutely not."

Anger filled him to the brim at the idea she'd sell herself to the highest bidder. And what goon from her dating past would be the lucky lotto winner? The idea of Stefanie being taken advantage of again made his blood pressure climb to dangerous levels.

"Listen. It's a surefire plan. This is the ultimate undo button for me. Haven't you ever wanted to go back in time and stop a tragedy from happening?"

Her pulled-up blond hair revealed a sweet face silhouetted by the cheesy town holiday decorations and winking lights in every window of city hall. Hell yes, he'd wanted to go back in time. He'd fantasized about going back for a huge "undo" for most of his childhood life.

"Yes," he answered honestly. She beamed, but that grin was erased when he spoke again. "Then I grew up and learned that what's done is done. There is no going back. There is no undo button on tragedy."

She squeezed his fingers as if apologizing for the tragic evening that changed his and his father's lives forever. She had no idea what had happened to him and his family—no one did. Save Chase, but Emmett had sworn his best friend to secrecy.

"Help me, Emmett. I'm begging." Against his will, the plea in her eyes took root in his chest. "You know it's serious if I have to beg. If there were anyone else, I'd ask them. But there's only you."

The sentiment was strange to hear in any context, especially in one where he was being proposed to, but it didn't stop him from reconsidering.

"I'm not going in there," he said. Stefanie's shoulders slumped in defeat before he added, "Until you explain every last detail of how this will work."

Thirty minutes later Stefanie walked out of city hall with her fiancé.

Her big, brawny, silent, scowling fiancé.

"There." She pointed across the street at a jeweler and marched over as soon as there was a break in traffic. She was a woman on a mission.

A cheery bell jingled as she pushed open the door of the jewelry store. Emmett did a neat jog to catch up and join her, but his expression remained as unreadable as it had when they'd applied for their marriage license.

It was so simple it was sort of unbelievable. It was like they'd let anyone get married these days.

"Hello." A saleslady scanned her new customers, ring-laden fingers clasped at her front. "What can I help you find today?"

"Wedding bands. And an engagement ring."

"Congratulations."

"Thanks." Stef peeked over her shoulder at Emmett, who was standing by the door looking unhappy.

She jerked her head, widening her eyes to communicate her meaning: *get your ass in here.*

He strode in, a reluctant lurch to his walk, as the saleslady led them to a glass case filled with sparkling diamond bands. She pulled out a tray of platinum settings at Stefanie's request. Stef leaned over them, fingering each one.

"They're beautiful."

She reached for a princess cut but before she had it lifted from its velvet bed, Emmett pushed the ring back down and plucked a band featuring a trio of marquise-cut diamonds instead. Rows of smaller diamonds winked from their homes on each side of the band.

"Great choice," the saleslady praised. "That's an old set. It was traded in yesterday by a woman whose husband passed away ten years ago. They were married forty-eight years and she had no children to leave it to. She said their marriage was a happy one, but she was re-marrying and felt wrong keeping it. She thought bringing it here would allow another couple to give it new life for another four decades or more." She eyed Emmett and then Stefanie. "You two look young enough to make it to your forty-eighth wedding anniversary."

It was both a sad and sweet sentiment since Stef knew that her marriage to Emmett wouldn't last until summer.

"Go ahead and slip it onto her finger," the saleslady told Emmett with a wink. "Practice for the big day."

He lifted Stef's left hand, the ring gripped between his blunt fingers.

"Maybe this ring is the wrong choice for us." She started to tug her hand away, but her betrothed didn't heed her warning, instead slipping the ring past her third finger's knuckles, where it sat as snugly as if it'd been sized for her hand.

"It's perfect." His gruff voice held a note of surprise.

"It's beautiful." The saleslady took Stefanie's hand and turned the diamond this way and that. "I tightened those prongs myself."

It was beautiful. And Emmett was right. It was also perfect. The woman handed over the matching band, and he pulled it onto his finger—again, a perfect fit.

"It was meant to be." The saleslady let out a gasp of delight. "We have financing and we also accept credit cards."

"Cash." Emmett wiggled the ring from his finger and placed it onto the counter as Stef was reaching into her purse for her wallet.

"Splendid. Let me grab a few boxes." The saleslady dashed off to the back, rings in hand and a spring in her step thanks to the hefty price tag.

"I'll pay for it," Stef said.

"No. You won't."

"Em—"

"Let me." He grasped her hand where the engagement ring sat, his palm big and warm. An answering warmth curled around her heart and sent a flush up her neck.

Speechless, she let Emmett take care of the purchase.

Six

Emmett drew the line at shopping for clothes.

Applying for a marriage license and purchasing the rings they'd exchange during their vows had been surreal enough. If she added a wedding dress to the mix, he'd have to call a shrink.

Agreeing to her harebrained plan would work twofold. It would defuse the threat to Chase's campaign and keep Stefanie out of one of her boneheaded exes' beds.

Emmett couldn't stomach the idea of her stooping to offer herself to another man who likely had his sights set on the Ferguson fortune. Not when Emmett himself was perfectly able to fill the role of temporary husband—and would sooner die than be compensated for the task.

He'd slid that band onto Stefanie's finger in the jewelry store, the tale of the ring's past eating into his soul. What he hadn't been able to deny was his desire to protect her at all costs. The rest of the Fergusons weren't going to approve, but Emmett didn't care. Stefanie needed him, and in the same way he'd been protecting the Ferguson family since Chase hired Emmett onto the security team, he'd protect Stef now. She didn't need him to leap in front of a bullet. She needed him to commit to a vow that was temporary for both of them.

He could hardly believe he'd let her talk him into it.

"There it is." She pointed out the window at a tall Victorian home. The painted wood siding was slate with brick red shutters. The matching sign was dusted with a thin layer of snow and the wood-carved lettering read Lawson Bed and Breakfast. "It's as pretty as the online photos."

It was a regal house in an older neighborhood of Harlington, probably from before the oil wells dried up, back when the residents believed it to be a forever home. It was impressive that it'd been kept up. He pulled down the driveway and into a parking area with four spots. Three of which were taken.

"Margaret Lawson runs the B and B," Stef said as they walked to the front door. She rang the buzzer. "Her son will be officiating our wedding. We'll have to share a room, I'm afraid. Otherwise, it'd look weird."

"Gee, I'd hate to look weird." He caught sight of the engagement ring when she tugged off one glove, then the next. It was odd seeing it there—the ring he'd *put* there. It filled him with a propriety he had no right to feel. As if she were *his* to care for and watch over.

A cheery redhead answered the door. "You must be Stefanie. And this is your…"

"Emmett Keaton." He thrust a hand forward in introduction.

"Nice to meet you. Your room is ready whenever you are."

"Is there a couch or extra bed in our room?" he blurted. When Margaret's smile vanished, he covered with "I toss and turn. Wouldn't want my future missus to lose any beauty sleep."

The older woman glanced from Emmett to Stefanie, who was regarding him like she wanted to strangle him.

"There's a love seat," Margaret answered. "A rather small one."

"We'll make do. Thank you, Margaret," Stef said. "Honey, won't you grab the luggage?"

He could take a hint. He excused himself to unload the SUV as Stefanie followed their hostess into the house.

Granted, this was her idea, but could Emmett at least *appear* to like her? First, he argued that she was insane for suggesting a marriage of convenience, then he asked the owner of the B and B for separate sleeping accommodations. At least he'd been game for the ring buying or else she would have developed a complex.

He stomped into the room in heavy boots and unloaded their luggage—several bags for her and one duffel bag for him.

"Do you have a suit and tie in there?" she asked.

"I have what you see me wearing in there." He unshouldered his coat to reveal his white-shirt-black-pants combo. His broad frame filled the room—which was small by anyone's definition of the word. Having him in it shrank it to cracker-box size.

She tapped a key on her laptop, having extracted the computer from her bag first. "I'll look into tux rental."

"What's it matter?"

From her cross-legged seat on the center of the bed, she slapped the laptop closed. In a voice low but firm, she told him exactly why it mattered.

"This isn't going to work unless you pretend to at least like me. I've been doing a good job of cordiality but you are failing with a capital *F*. Margaret patted me on the arm after leading me up here and assured me men always behaved strangely before a wedding and not to take what you said to heart!"

"I don't see how that is any of her business."

"I don't see how you're missing the point I'm so clearly conveying," she snapped. Closing her eyes, she pulled in a deep breath. *Serenity now!* "We need everyone to buy into the farce or else it'll leak that this is fake, which will give Blake even more ammunition and ruin my reputation."

"What do you suggest I do, Stef? Follow you around like a puppy? Hold your hand? Nuzzle your neck?" he bit out.

The idea of Emmett holding her close and nuzzling her *anything* had her growing warm—and not in a good way. She'd obligated him enough. She couldn't ask that he force a reaction he wasn't comfortable with. That would be sexual harassment.

"Of course not." She craned her chin as he stepped closer to the bed.

He folded his arms over his chest and looked down at her, his weighty presence stifling and strangely sensual. Flummoxed by her reaction to him, she changed the subject.

"I have errands to run over the next couple of days. Wedding dress and shoe shopping."

She also needed to go to the site of the charity dinner and make sure everything was coming along as planned. Caterers would be delivering tables and chairs, and decorating no fewer than three Christmas trees. Not to mention that the volunteers from the community church would be wrapping presents for the invited families.

"I'll need you to drive me." She half expected resistance but Emmett nodded easily. "I won't make you wear a tux."

"Fine."

"Great."

"Great."

He eyed the bed where she was sitting, legs folded pretzel-style in front of her. Then he sent a glance at the diminutive love seat on the other side of the room.

"You can have the bed," she told him. "I'll sleep on the couch."

"Nice try." He grinned, an almost jovial light in his eyes. It faded as fast as it appeared, but damn, what she wouldn't give to see it again. That smile had transformed his entire face. "I'll take the floor."

"It's cold down there."

"I'll live." He walked to the door and when she asked where he was going, he turned to answer her, his body taking up most of the doorway. "I have a sleeping bag in the SUV, Stef. Stop worrying about me, yeah?"

Then he patted the doorway and was off.

She wasn't worrying about him, but she was trying to accommodate him. Clearly, he was uncomfortable, and now that they were to be wedded she was feeling equally awkward about their suddenly intimate situation. How was she going to manage an "I do" kiss and sharing a room with him if she could barely talk to him when they were alone?

And it wouldn't end in Harlington.

No, this decision would follow her home. Follow her around until she and Emmett were *un*married. And what would they do until then?

She didn't want to think about it. She opened her laptop and started typing a list of to-dos for her wedding. After a few minutes of crafting a list, she realized that even the basics were going to take plenty of time and energy and effort.

In order to pull off a wedding as well as a successful charity dinner, she would have to either make a clone of herself or do some delegating. And there was only one other person to delegate *to*.

That person strode back into the room with a rolled sleeping bag tucked under his arm. He hadn't bothered with his coat for the quick jaunt outside, so his face and nose were red even from the brief exposure. Before he dropped the bag, she made her request.

"I need your help with a few things while I'm here." Realizing that sounded demanding, she added, "If you can take the time away from your job."

"You are my job while I'm here." He crossed the room and dumped the sleeping bag onto the love seat.

It was easier for her to admit this next part while looking at his back…

"One more thing…" He turned before she could finish and she gulped, a dry sound that caused her throat to click. "I need to tell you the truth about why we're here."

Seven

"You mean there's more to it than cornering me into matrimony and eating a fancy dinner with your fancy friends?"

But that last bit didn't make much sense, did it? Not now that they were in Harlington, where the "fanciest" restaurant in town was a Chili's.

"You're joking with me. That's new. Usually you're frowning at me." Her smile was tentative. She leaned back on the bed, the pair of leggings making her slim legs look a mile long and the oversize pink sweater hiding her petite curves. She looked comfortable and relaxed, which was as crazy as the fact that he felt the same way.

Stefanie didn't like him—he'd have lost a bet that she'd smile at him let alone *propose* to him even if it were up to them to repopulate the planet. There were a million strings attached to the proposal, and it was an arrangement for the greater good, but…shouldn't they both be more on edge?

She picked at a thread on the quilt rather than look up at him. "Does this mean we're becoming friendly instead of mortal enemies? That someday I could be more than a job to you?"

Ah, hell. Surely she didn't think that. He didn't consider her an enemy—he liked her.

He cared about her safety.

And about her as a person.

"I only ask because we need to make this marriage look real if we go forward. How good of an actor are you?"

His face scrunched at the question.

"Can you hold my hand in public? Open a door for me? Be a gentleman? I don't think the public would believe I'd fall for someone who didn't do those things."

"Who cares what the public thinks?" he barked, stung at her accusing him of not knowing how to treat a woman. He was accustomed to protecting—to watching other people's backs. That was why he brought up the rear whenever they walked anywhere together.

"Do it for Chase if you can't do it for me." Hurt flooded her eyes.

Did she really believe he found her so unsavory? Emmett wouldn't stoop to defend himself aloud, but his thoughts went there. He *was* doing this for her. So that she could come out here to…do whatever she was doing.

"You owe me the truth," he reminded her. But when she took a breath, presumably to tell him, he held up a hand. "Not here, though. I'm hungry."

Stefanie had never set foot inside a Chili's restaurant until today. It wasn't that she was too good for a burger and fries; it was that there wasn't much of an opportunity to go to a chain when there were hundreds of other unique restaurants to choose from. Any man she'd dated had endeavored to impress her with meals that had cost hundreds of dollars.

Emmett didn't apologize for choosing a restaurant that had nary a word of French on the menu. She appreciated being treated as an equal and not catered to like some spoiled rich girl. She wasn't sure if it was because he was stubborn or because he knew her better than anyone else, but the latter seemed impossible. They barely knew each other at all.

Once they were settled in with their drinks—wine for her and beer for him—and a bowl of warm tortilla chips and a dish of salsa, Emmett gestured with a chip for her to speak. "Go."

"I'm not in Harlington for a girls' getaway."

"I gathered." He piled salsa onto another chip.

"For the last three years I've been hosting charity dinners for families who can't afford a Christmas on their own." She reached for her wine, her throat dry. "I'm planning on taking it public next year, maybe recruit some 'elves' to help me throw more than one charity dinner at a time. I guess I'm saying…this will be my last year for anonymity."

He said nothing, regarding her with a narrowed gaze. Stefanie could understand why. It probably didn't make sense to him why she would keep a noble cause quiet.

"I wanted to do it on my own," she supplied. "In case you haven't noticed, my parents and two older brothers, not to mention my oldest brother's best friend—" she paused to give him a meaningful eyebrow raise "—don't let me do much on my own. I don't want anyone's input. Succeed or fail, I wanted the outcome on me.

"It's been a success. I've hired assistants over the years to help me pull it off, but I do most of the work. I'm a party planner and an organizer by nature. It's a challenge I enjoy."

Emmett crunched another chip as if she hadn't revealed a huge secret or exposed her tender underbelly to him. Either he was too hungry to comment or…

Well, she didn't know *or what*.

Guessing what was inside his head was a challenge she was not equipped for.

"Say something."

After a long guzzle of beer, he did. "You provide Christmas dinner for poor people."

"And gifts. That's simplifying it, but yes. The idea that a little boy or girl wouldn't wake up to gifts or a Christmas tree made me want to change all of that. I've always had magical Christmases. I couldn't imagine not having them."

He nodded, but the reaction was noncommittal at best. Not that she wanted praise for her charitable work, but she had expected a more favorable reaction. She'd always assumed Emmett considered her the shallow end of the Ferguson gene pool. Much as she'd convinced herself she didn't care what he thought of her, she did. It was her plight.

In a dark corner of her heart, she cared what a great many people thought of her.

"You'll be glad to know that your standard attire for work is acceptable for the dinner."

"I'm not going."

She blinked at his reaction.

"You're my fiancé. Of course you're going. What else are you going to do?" She tried a tactic she was sure would sway him in her favor—making him believe she could be in danger at the event. "I never know what kind of people could show up, so it would be nice if you were watching out for me and the volunteers. I won't make you talk to anybody. You can be your lovely, quiet, unsociable self."

He sat back in the booth and crossed his thick arms over his thicker chest.

"I bet you would enjoy it. It's rewarding to give back to those who have little when you have so much."

Since she was looking right at him she didn't miss one of his eyes twitching or the frown between his eyebrows deepening.

She didn't understand. What kind of person wouldn't support a charity that provided Christmas for underprivileged kids? Had she pegged Emmett wrong? Was he truly the scrooge she'd labeled him as?

"Anyway…" she said when it was clear he wasn't going to say another word. "Now you know the real reason I'm here. And it's not to gallivant with my friends. I'll just gallivant with you instead."

It was like delivering a speech to a stone wall…one that ate chips and salsa.

"You'd be pretty if you smiled more." She batted her eyelashes coyly, but Emmett didn't smile. "Yeah, that line never works when a man says it to me, either." She reached for a chip and shrugged, giving up.

After dinner, they returned to the B and B, where they passed Margaret in the kitchen. Their hostess was pouring steaming mulled cider into red and green mugs.

"Emmett and Stefanie!" she greeted. "Your timing is perfect. I was about to take a tray of drinks into the living room. There's a fire in the fireplace, pine garlands draped over every surface and Christmas music playing."

"That sounds absolutely dreamy." Stefanie inhaled the scent of warmed cinnamon and clove and citrusy orange rind. "Let me take my purse upstairs and we'll be right down."

Around the corner at the stairs, she stopped on the second step, alarmed to feel Emmett's palm at her lower back. She turned and regarded him curiously.

"Isn't this a gentlemanly thing to do?"

"Unless you are trying to steady me because I had a second glass of wine, then yes." She had to smile as she ascended the steps, his hand on her lower back before it slipped casually to her hip.

He'd been listening to her, after all.

He'd also opened the door for her when they exited Chili's, and then he made a point not to unlock the SUV so he could open that door for her, as well.

The conversation at dinner had been mostly one-sided as she'd chattered about the charity. She was trying to be friendly, but it was hard to be friendly with someone who…was introverted? Didn't know how to be friendly? She had no idea what Emmett's issue was, and she was tired of guessing.

Tonight, she'd enjoy warm cider and Christmas music in front of a crackling fire.

In their shared room, she hung her coat on a hook on the wall and deposited her purse on the bed. When she turned and found Emmett untying his boots, she asked, "Why are you taking off your shoes? We're going to the living room."

"Pass."

"Emmett. We're engaged. People expect to see us together."

"People get tired. You can tell them that's what happened to me." He took off his other boot and dropped it with a *thunk*.

"This is a perfect opportunity for you to practice being with me around people."

He let out a grunt before standing in front of her. Almost *over* her. He took a step closer, his hand going to the shiny metal buckle of his belt. She watched as he pulled the thick leather through the buckle and she licked her lips, her mouth practically watering. It took everything in her not to drop her attention to his waist or lower.

"What are you doing?" she croaked when he reached for the button on his slacks.

"I'm going to take a shower. And then I'm going to bed."

"How about one mug of cider?" She tried again, blinking out of the pheromone haze saturating the air between them.

"Knock yourself out. I'm not going down there." His eyes on hers, he slowly pulled the belt through the loops of his pants and began rolling it.

Was it hot in here or was it just him?

When he reached for his zipper, she shut her eyes.

"Can you at least wait until I leave the room?"

"Aren't we supposed to be practicing?"

Her eyes flew open, her cheeks heating with… something. Lust? Frustration? Frustrated lust?

But before she could take him to task, she saw one corner of his mouth lift in amusement.

"Thought you liked it when I joked."

"All joking aside—" she cleared her throat "—there's no need to practice the physical part."

"You sure? A lengthy kiss usually follows the 'I dos.'"

"I'm pretty sure I can wing a chaste marital kiss. Even with you."

"You're the boss."

His gaze drifted to her mouth, that move as sensual as if he'd leaned forward to press his lips to hers.

"Right. I'll be back up in an hour."

"Take your time."

She fished her room key out of her purse as she heard the rustle of clothing that—she guessed—was Emmett taking off his pants. Hand sweating on the knob, she exited and walked into the hallway, shutting their bedroom door behind her. No way was she turning around to see if he was a boxers or briefs guy.

No freaking way.

Eight

Emmett was lying on the hard floor, the thin carpeting doing his back no favors. And the sleeping bag wasn't helping after a long day of driving, getting engaged and the bonus of being pummeled by memories.

Stef had gone downstairs well over an hour ago, and now his little social butterfly was taking her sweet time delighting the guests of Lawson B and B. He could imagine her broad, infectious smile. The way she stood when she told a joke and almost always flubbed the ending.

He closed his eyes and shook his head, wishing she'd come back if for no other reason than to distract him. He could go downstairs, he supposed, but after he'd found out the real reason for her being in Harlington, something inside him had cracked open and out seeped decades of toxic waste.

He'd been in one of those families she was planning on serving. After his mother and baby brother had passed away, his father quit working. They'd had financial help from the state, and his old man had qualified for disability thanks to an unsuccessful attempt at suicide.

That'd been a shitty Christmas.

Emmett had worked hard to escape his past, to make up for the assistance his father sponged off the system. He'd done well for himself, and always worked harder than expected to make sure he earned every cent of his paycheck. As his check was signed by a Ferguson, it was no surprise that Stef's sharing that she was in town to help the less fortunate had struck a raw chord.

As if he needed a reminder that she was better than him in every way.

Uglier thoughts like that one had traipsed around his mind in a demented square dance since he'd climbed out of the shower. Thoughts like, if Chase knew who he really was, would they even be friends? Emmett had shared everything with his best bud save what income bracket he'd hailed from. He'd also wondered if Stefanie ever would have approached him about marrying her if she knew he'd once qualified to be one of the guests at her dinner.

The entire scenario sickened him. He couldn't escape the loss that came back like the Ghost of Christmas Past. He couldn't shake the feeling that he was a sheep in wolf's clothing—and underneath the tough exterior was a tender boy with a broken heart.

"Fucking Christmas." He pushed himself to sitting, ran a hand over his short hair and sighed. Sleep was so far away he'd need a passport to get there.

Dressed in only boxer briefs and a sleeveless tank, he braced himself against the chill in the room when he climbed to his feet. The Victorian was an old house and drafty as hell.

He knelt to check the fridge beneath the television, praying for a few of those miniature overpriced bottles of booze to take the edge off. He never made a habit of drinking away a mood, but in this case, it would serve a dual purpose. He'd warm up, too.

He inspected the fridge's contents—OJ, milk and water. Not a bottle of liquor to be found.

The sound of a key card sliding through the pad drew his attention to the door. Stefanie stepped into the room, her smile slightly wonky but no less charming. She carried two steaming mugs.

"I was hoping you'd be awake." She smiled brightly, and even in the meager light leaking in from the streetlamp through the lace curtains he could see the pink tinge of her cheeks. "I had Margaret heat up a few more of these—and add some bourbon." She bared her teeth in a bright grin. "I've already had one with bourbon."

In spite of all that had haunted him this evening, he felt better already. She'd walked into the room and her presence had slain the demons.

"I'll take it." He flicked on a nearby lamp. "Nothing but nonalcoholic beverages in the room."

"Well then. You're welcome." She handed over the cider topped with whipped cream. He wasn't sure this concoction would make a difference in his mood, but it was worth a shot.

She sipped and then licked the whipped cream off her upper lip. At the same time, they moved to sit on the end of the bed.

"Sorry," she said.

"Go ahead." He gestured, remaining standing.

She sat, patting the bedding next to her. He regarded the quilt for a beat before easing down next to her.

Curling her legs beneath her, she held the mug with both hands and hummed. "I love being warm."

"In this drafty house that might be a challenge. I didn't see a thermostat in this room."

Her eyes went past him to his bed on the floor. "Is it cold down there?"

He shrugged.

"You could always—"

"It's fine." Whatever she was about to suggest, he couldn't let her. She wasn't sleeping down there—or wedging herself onto the tiny sofa.

He drank his cider carefully to make sure it wasn't too hot. It was perfect, and the sweet tang of bourbon welcome.

"Margaret has the hearth decorated with thick greenery and gold ribbon. Glass-and-glitter ornaments and nutcrackers that her children buy her every year." Stef's eyes were bright and happy. "Don't you love Christmas?"

He nearly choked on his next sip.

"No." He wasn't sure what possessed him to tell the truth, but there it was.

"At all?" She regarded him like he'd announced he kicked puppies in his spare time.

"Not at all."

"Why?"

He turned to face her and was struck dumb by the blue of her eyes. Stefanie Ferguson was a beautiful woman. He'd noticed before—it was impossible not to notice—but until now he'd never given himself the luxury to truly look at her.

She was royalty and he was more like a stable boy.

In his mind, there'd never been a misconception about who she was and who he was—where she hailed from versus the rock he'd crawled out from under. She was whole, and he'd lost a chunk of himself a long time ago. Whatever passing admiration he'd felt for her in the past, he'd shut it down immediately.

"Did something bad happen?" she pushed.

"Yes." He cleared his throat and stood, setting aside his warm drink, the whipped cream melted.

"Will you tell me about it?"

He faced her, hyperaware that she was dressed from head to toe and he was in his underwear. She noticed, too. He watched her take him in, her eyes sliding down his chest and lower.

Interesting.

Had she ever looked at him with anything other than disdain?

"It's not a happy story, Stef. I'd rather let you keep your delusions that Christmas is magical and wondrous."

A line formed between her eyebrows. "I'm not a child because I choose to see the good. Why not admit you're too much of a coward to share what's bugging you rather than lash out at me?"

Ah, familiar ground. With a sigh, he returned to the bed, arms resting in his lap. Maybe she was right. Maybe he was lashing out. His blurred reflection watched him from the dark television's screen. His broad shoulders were slumped as he sat there like a stubborn giant. Stefanie sat delicate as a fairy, blond hair out of its ponytail and spilling over her shoulders, her chin down as she watched him through her lashes.

They were contrasting in every way.

The filthy-rich girl. The wrong-side-of-the-tracks guy. She'd been blessed by the gods and his luck always felt like it was on the verge of running out. He didn't talk about his family tragedy for a lot of reasons, the dominating one being habit.

"Fine. Don't tell me." She stood and set her mug aside, but before she could huff off to the attached bathroom, he wrapped his fingers around her arm. Her eyes widened.

"Sorry." He held up both hands. "I didn't mean to—"

Rather than finish the thought, he scrubbed a palm over his short hair. "If you really want to know, I'll tell you."

Arms crossed, she hoisted an eyebrow in a proprietary manner and waited.

The floor was his.

Standing over Emmett was an odd juxtaposition.

She'd never seen him like this. In his underpants, sure, but she'd also never seen him look so...tired.

She had the irrational urge to touch him. She curled her fingers into fists to keep from reaching for him.

How could he not like Christmas?

"It was a long time ago," he started.

Her stomach tightened at his foreboding tone. She'd wondered at first if he'd suffered a bad breakup over the holidays, but the hollowness in his voice suggested this tale was much, much worse than a broken heart.

"I was...six years old." He palmed the back of his neck, clearly uncomfortable sharing this story. "My dad and I went out. I can't remember why. The grocery store, maybe? Gas station? Whatever was open at 6:00 a.m. on Christmas morning."

His throat bobbed as he swallowed, his gaze unfocused on a spot across the room.

"We returned to our street and fire engines were

lining both sides of it. Police cars wouldn't let us close, so my dad climbed out of the truck and busted through the cops to see what happened."

He sighed and paused as if gathering the strength to continue.

"The house was a total loss. My mom and my baby brother, Michael, didn't survive the fire. They said later it was caused by faulty wiring." The tilt of his lips was dark, humorless. "Half my family...gone, thanks to a shoddy electrician."

She let out a sound between a whimper and a gasp. What a horrible tragedy.

"I don't remember a lot from that day. More what happened in the years that followed. Sadness hovered in our apartment like a gas leak. There was no escaping. Until I did."

"Oh, Emmett." She gave in and sat, grabbing his hand, holding it with both of hers. He stiffened next to her, his arm going taut, his expression unreadable.

He shrugged one shoulder as if to assure her it was okay, but it wasn't okay, was it? Losing a parent and a brother in a house fire when you were six years old could never be okay.

She stroked her hand up his arm in an attempt to warm him, or maybe warm herself. Since he'd spoken it was as if a chill had come over the room. Like a ghost had passed by them both.

Or two ghosts.

She shivered.

"Like I said, it was a long time ago."

Still. It wasn't like losing half your family was easily forgotten. And he'd been a little boy.

"Anyway." He straightened his back, pushing the conversation aside. "Dad never was much of a Christmas guy, and I followed suit. And I'm not big on strings of cheap lights in my house decorating a highly flammable dead tree."

His hand was still in hers and she squeezed his palm.

"It was an awful tragedy, Emmett. I'm so sorry."

He faced her, his expression younger somehow, or maybe lighter. Like unburdening that story had taken years off him.

"I don't normally share that."

"I understand why." Who would want to relive that pain?

His eyes dipped briefly to her lips, igniting a sizzle in the air that had no place being there after he'd shared the sad story of his past. Even so, her answering reaction was to study his firm mouth in contemplation. The barely-there scruff lining his angled jaw. His dominating presence made her feel fragile yet safe at the same time.

The urge to comfort him—to comfort herself— lingered. This time she didn't deny it.

With her free hand, she reached up and cupped the thick column of his neck, tugging him down. He resisted, but only barely, stopping short a brief distance from her mouth to mutter one word.

"Hey…"

She didn't know if he'd meant to follow it with "This is a bad idea" or "We shouldn't get carried away," but she didn't wait to find out.

Her lips touched his gently and his mouth answered by puckering to return the kiss. Her eyes sank closed and his hand flinched against her palm.

He tasted…*amazing*. Like spiced cider and a capable, strong, heartbroken man who kept his hurts hidden from the outside world.

Eyes closed, she gripped the back of his neck tighter,

angling her head to get more of his mouth. And when he pulled his hand from hers to come to rest on her shoulder, she swore she might melt from that casual touch. His tongue came out to play, tangling with hers in a sensual, forbidden dance.

She fisted his undershirt, tugging it up and brushing against the plane of his firm abs, and Emmett's response was to lift the hem of her sweater, where his rough fingertips touched the exposed skin of her torso.

A tight, needy sound escaped her throat, and his lips abruptly stopped moving against hers.

He pulled back, blinking at her with lust-heavy lids. She touched her mouth and looked away, the heady spell broken.

She'd just kissed her brother's best friend—a man who until today she might have jokingly described as her mortal enemy.

Worse, Emmett had kissed her back.

It was okay for this to be pretend—for their wedding to be an arrangement, but there was nothing black-and-white between them any longer. There was real attraction—as volatile as a live wire and as dangerous as a downed electric pole.

Whatever line they'd drawn by agreeing to marry, she'd stepped way, *way* over it.

He sobered quickly, recovering faster than she did. When he spoke, he echoed the words in her mind.

"That was a mistake."

Nine

The following two days passed in a flurry of activity.

Stefanie didn't take the time to sit around and wonder what motivation lurked beneath her kissing Emmett, and she certainly didn't give any brain space as to why he'd kissed her back.

Until this morning.

She'd slipped into the bathroom and showered, replaying the kiss and Emmett's reaction to it. He wasn't wrong. It had been a mistake to kiss him. And yet she'd wanted to kiss him again ever since. She had the tendency to lean in whenever she felt the urge, and that night she'd *literally* leaned in.

After climbing out of the shower she blow-dried her hair, her mind a tangle of confusion. Mostly because kissing Emmett had felt undeniably right when it shouldn't have felt anything less than…wrong.

With no resolution in sight, she tabled the thoughts

and set out from the B and B with a list and Emmett in tow. She had plans to finalize not only for the charity Christmas dinner but also for the wedding in which she was one of the main participants.

She could hardly believe she was going to be married tonight.

"May I help you?" a pretty dark-haired woman at the counter of the bridal boutique asked.

"Yes, I purchased a Vera Wang wedding dress yesterday and paid extra to have it taken in by today."

The small boutique in San Antonio had displayed the Vera Wang on a mannequin in a glass case under lock and key. It was one of a kind, and exactly the type of wedding dress she would've picked out for a real wedding. Not that this wasn't real, but she wasn't in love, so that made it *less* real.

"Tonight's my wedding night."

"Congratulations!"

But announcing it hadn't made it any less surreal.

"Sandy Phillips." An older woman emerged from the back and greeted Stefanie using her alias. The last thing Stef needed was word leaking to the media that she was buying a wedding gown. "Danielle, could you please pull the vintage Vera Wang for Ms. Phillips?"

"Of course." Danielle vanished behind a curtain and Nancy, who was also the owner of the store, patted Stef's hand.

"Are you excited? It's the big day!"

If by excited she meant nauseous and ready to get it over with, then yes. Yes, she was.

"Very."

"Is that your beau out front?"

Stefanie turned to the wide plate glass window. Emmett's SUV idled at the curb, the passenger-side window cracked, probably to release some of the warmth from the cab. He'd accused her of "cooking him" by turning up the heat on the passenger side, but she couldn't help it that San Antonio was suffering a cold spell.

"That's him."

"Yum." Nancy gave her a conspiratorial wink.

After Stef had slipped into her dress to ensure the alterations were perfect—they were—she carried her dress to the car and draped the opaque black bag over the back seat.

"Need help?" Emmett asked over his shoulder.

"No. I have it." She closed the back door, then opened her own, climbing inside and buckling up. At least the sun was out today. The snow had turned into rain and what white stuff was decorating the ground and windowsills had melted away. "That's the last item on my to-do list."

As he pulled onto the highway, she spotted a Starbucks sign on the horizon, and her mouth watered for a cinnamony, nutmeggy, sugary concoction.

"Coffee!" she exclaimed. "Coffee and then I'm done with my to-do list."

"Here?" He pointed at a fast-food place as they passed by. At her aghast reaction, he chuckled, the sound low and comforting. "Kidding."

The thirty-minute drive back to the B and B was quiet, mostly because she was cocooning a toasted-marshmallow white-chocolate mocha. Seriously. So good.

"Is this how you imagined your wedding day?" Emmett broke the silence, glanced in the rearview and changed lanes smoothly.

"Every detail. Right down to the mocha and a fiancé I had to beg to enter with me into holy matrimony." She smiled and he returned it, holding her gaze for a beat before he put his eyes on the road again.

An odd ripple of comfort spilled down her spine. How was it that he made this outrageous situation seem normal?

And how strange was it that she was proud to have chosen him as her groom, and relieved that he'd said yes to her proposal?

Emmett had experienced many catered charity dinners as a kid. Up close and way too personal. More than a few times his father had dragged him to a local church that hosted Christmas dinners for the "needy." Emmett had always hated that word. To him, it implied that he was taking what he hadn't earned, even though the parishioners never made them feel anything less than welcome.

He remembered wearing his coat to fend off a draft in a dusty gymnasium and squeezing in with strangers and no elbow room at a battered plywood banquet table. Not that he hadn't appreciated the efforts of the volunteers serving those dinners—he had. But the food had always been accompanied by a hefty dose of shame. He'd kept his ball cap pulled low and his head down, fearing he'd run into someone he knew.

He'd vowed, while eating many meals of oversalted vegetables and tough meat, that the very second he was old enough to find a job, he would. *And* he'd make enough money to eat Christmas dinner at his own table in his own house. He'd never liked being served, and it took him several years to warm to the idea of going out to restaurants.

But setting foot inside the venue Stefanie had prepared for her charity dinner didn't bring back memories of those days. Mainly because the venue was nothing like the dusty gym packed with wobbly tables.

The former banquet hall and restaurant had been maintained by a private owner in Harlington for rental during special occasions. Unlike a YMCA or gymnasium, the room was outfitted with wide round tables covered with shimmery gold tablecloths. The entire setup—from the elegant white plates to the stemware and the regal centerpieces of pinecones and white flowers—reminded him of a fancy Ferguson affair.

"What do you think?" Stefanie looked up at him, her grin proud.

He nodded, and then figured that after her hard work she deserved an actual compliment. "I'm impressed."

"Thanks!" She skipped off to the catering staff and another gaggle of people he assumed to be volunteers.

Hosting a party. Yeah, she was in her element all right.

The families had yet to arrive, but everyone else was in place. Volunteers dressed in T-shirts emblazoned with the words HARLINGTON CARES waited at the mouth of what Emmett assumed was the kitchen—no buffet setup here. Stefanie directed a few of the volunteers toward different points around the room. Three enormous trees dripped with ornaments and were surrounded by teetering stacks of wrapped gifts.

The air smelled of roasted meat and underlying scents of herbs and butter. Emmett's stomach rumbled. Lunch had happened too long ago, especially now that his nose had caught a hint of what awaited him.

"Hey, this is where we're sitting." Stef grabbed his hand and tugged him to a table in the rear of the room, near one of the trees. A metal sign in the center read VOLUNTEERS.

"I'm here as your security guy, not a guest," he said as his stomach clenched in protest.

"Hank and Albert over there are police officers, so you may stand down. Besides, what better way to protect me than sitting by my side?" She leaned in, her hand still warming his. "And it's your last chance to eat and gather your strength before our wedding."

At the reminder of what was to come tonight, his stomach clenched for an entirely different reason. Her beautiful blue eyes, flaxen hair and indelible smile hadn't changed, but since he'd allowed himself to taste those lips, the way he saw her *had* changed. No longer was she the untouchable sister of the mayor. Not since she'd touched him and he'd touched her back. The idea of having her as his had taken root and, without his permission, had outgrown Jack's bean stalk.

He'd felt the burn of lust for her since that unexpected kiss, and after they exchanged vows, he'd be damned if he'd back off.

There was only one way to go with this woman, and that was forward.

"You're the one who'd better gather your strength." He leaned in, his breath warming her ear. "Tonight I'm not sleeping on the cold floor alone."

Her mouth dropped open but no words came out.

"What we do in bed is your call." This close to her he could watch as her pupils darkened. "But we're sharing the covers tonight."

"I thought—" she blinked a few times until she found the rest of that sentence "—the kiss was a mistake."

Yeah, well. He'd thought it was, too.

And then they spent the next two days together and all he could think about was taking her lips captive again. Running his fingers into her soft hair this time, tilting her head and stroking her tongue with his...

Easy.

Last thing he needed was to get hard at a charity dinner.

"There's no taking it back now." There wasn't any forgetting it, either. Last night he'd lain awake in the chilled room wondering if Stef was awake, too, eyes on the ceiling, her mind on him. "You'll have to kiss me one more time before we return to our room. Together. On our wedding night."

"Your wedding night!" A plump, smiling, dark-skinned woman approached and wrapped Stefanie in a hug. "Sandy, you didn't tell me you were engaged! Introduce me!"

"Emmett, this is Lakesha. Lakesha, Emmett." Evidently there was no need for him to have a fake name.

"I've worked with Sandy for two years in a row and I love her to bits and pieces. Probably as much as you do." Lakesha shoved his chest and then squeezed one of his pecs. "Oh, and he's solid as a rock. Nicely done."

She high-fived Stef and Emmett snapped a look from one to the other. Never before had he been *high-fived* over. A reluctant smile itched the corner of his mouth.

Not only had Stef proposed to him, she'd initiated a kiss and now *claimed* him. He straightened his shoulders, forcing his posture into a stance that he hoped made him look like he belonged with her. A bizarrely heady thought since he knew he didn't.

Stef lowered her voice to just above a whisper. "Do me a favor and keep it under wraps. My family doesn't know yet."

Lakesha visibly bristled and peeked around to make

sure no one had overheard. Then pulled an invisible zipper over her lips and winked up at Emmett. "My lips are sealed."

Emmett watched his fiancée from the edge of the party, choosing to sandwich roasted turkey breast on a roll rather than sit down for dinner. The police officers who were working the event deserved to enjoy their meals.

Stef didn't sit much, either, hopping up to give a waiter direction or hustle off to the kitchen. He watched her stop at least six times in front of one of the Christmas trees to rearrange the donated presents, or fuss over bow or ribbon placement. She was ridiculously adorable. It was the first time he was able to watch her with unabashed admiration, no other eyes on him caring that he did, so he watched. Watched her with equal parts pride and wonder.

He'd known Stefanie in relation to Chase. He knew she was wild, quick-witted, sharp—and from observing her cry happy tears at Zach and Penelope's wedding, a romantic sap.

He smiled to himself at the thought. She was tender and open alongside headstrong and determined, and those combined traits made her even more attractive to him.

He could do a lot worse in the wife department. She could do a hell of a lot better in the husband one.

Even dressed down in black pants and a white sweater with sparkling gold thread woven into it, Stefanie Ferguson looked like royalty. Or at the very least a celebrity.

He couldn't believe no one had recognized her, but then he guessed she was mostly of interest to the city's elite. The good people of Harlington, Texas, had bigger priorities than a Dallas it girl. Working hard to provide for their families, putting food on the table and shopping for school clothes for their kids took a lot of focus and effort. He could relate.

After his mother and brother died, Emmett had taken on the role of parent. Van stopped caring, damn near stopped breathing. He mostly sat in front of the television, oxygen tank at his side and a glazed expression on his face courtesy of the prescription medication.

At age ten, Emmett had been as responsible as an adult. He'd mowed lawns, picked up groceries for his elderly neighbors and had let some of the smaller kids in school pay him to play bodyguard. Anything to bring in cash so he could put food in his belly and his father's.

A little girl approached Stefanie, a battered stuffed teddy bear in her arms, and Stef knelt to give her a hug. Her face was so genuine and her touch so light, his chest give a tug. She wasn't doing this for the publicity but for the people. He was beginning to see why she'd kept her secret, too. Chase talked to her as if he were in charge of her. As if she were a princess locked in a tower. Emmett could understand her desire to escape home and make her own way. He'd felt like that a lot growing up.

The remnants of dinner and dessert cleared, they moved on to the gift portion of the evening. A dressed Santa in red-and-white velvet was stationed at each tree handing out gifts to the kids.

Emmett watched from afar, sipping on a cup of cocoa delivered to him by Lakesha with another wink, a squeeze of his biceps and a "Congratulations, again!" And then something remarkable happened. He began to feel comfortable at the last place he should—at a charity dinner for the financially challenged…and as Stefanie's fiancé with only a few hours to go until they were husband and wife.

Ten

"That's new." Stefanie let out an uncomfortable laugh when she spotted what was hanging over the entrance of the B and B.

"What's new?" Emmett asked as he turned into the driveway.

"Mistletoe. Yikes."

"Thought you loved Christmas. Isn't mistletoe a holiday staple?"

"No." She had firm feelings about it and none of them were positive.

"No?" His tone was bemused. He parked, but let the engine idle, turning to face her in the dark cab of the SUV. "You're a romantic who loves Christmas and you don't put stock in the tradition of kissing beneath the mistletoe?"

"Well…neither do you, Scrooge. What's the big deal?"

"The *big deal* is that it makes sense for me because I hate Christmas, but you… It makes no sense."

They had a narrow-eyed standoff. "O Holy Night" played quietly on the radio alongside the gentle blow of heat from the vents.

"I told you my story. Tell me yours."

He had her there. On a sigh, she began the sordid tale.

"I was at a Christmas party with my parents when I was thirteen. This kid in my class—a piggish oaf named Reggie Meeks—grabbed me and kissed me underneath the mistletoe. Then he bragged to his stupid friends that I made out with him. Like, hot and heavy *made out*. Meanwhile, I ran into the nearest bathroom and swished with mouthwash until my teeth hurt."

Emmett chuckled.

"It's not funny!"

"You're right." He sobered some but his lips quirked as if he was hiding a smile. "He has an unfortunate name and it's not his fault."

She balled up her fist and punched Emmett's arm, which was like hitting a steel beam. She shook her hand out and frowned.

"I'm kidding." He took her hand and rubbed her knuckles, his palm warm and his eyes warmer. "It's *not* funny that a kid bullied you into a kiss. But holding a grudge against an innocent plant is criminal. You didn't make any new memories under the mistletoe after that?"

"Nope. One kiss from Reggie and I was scarred for life." She shuddered and this time Emmett's soft laughter didn't rankle her. "Thank you. For coming with me to the dinner. I could tell you didn't want to be there. I'm sure there was enough Christmas cheer in there to make you want to hide in a cave."

"It wasn't so bad." He let go of her hand and watched out the windshield, the attractive planes of his face highlighted in the dashboard lights.

He'd been through hell on Christmas Day, and he'd sworn off the happiest holiday because of it. He of all people should understand her grudge against kissing under mistletoe.

How about that? They had something in common.

Outside, the cold wind bit through her clothes and chilled her skin. Emmett walked beside her, head down, hands in his pockets.

"The big moment is fast approaching." He stopped at the bottom of three steps leading to the door. "You sure you want to do this?"

"Positive. I don't like being bullied. By Reggie Meeks *or* Blake Eastwood. I refuse to let Blake push me around like…" She trailed off, considering she might be doing the same to Emmett. Meeting his dark stare, she proceeded carefully. "Are you sure *you* want to do this? Are you feeling pressured? I'd never want to put you in a position—"

He cut off her words with a kiss before she knew what had hit her. His arm lashed against her lower back, he hauled her against the hard wall of his body and laid his lips on hers. The touch of his mouth to hers ignited sparks between them and suddenly the cold air didn't feel so cold.

Her gloveless fingers curled into the lapels of his coat and she dragged him closer, the scrape of the scruff on his chin chafing her sensitive skin. He finished the kiss with one brief stroke of his tongue before reverently kissing her top lip, then her bottom lip. He held her close as she inhaled a ragged breath and blew it out on a puff of steam. He cocked an eyebrow as if waiting for her reaction, but she couldn't muster up one save clinging to him like garland around a Christmas tree.

His eyes turned up and hers followed, to the mistletoe dangling overhead. When their gazes met again, he said, "Time for both of us to make better Christmas memories."

"Oh my heavens! I knew that mistletoe was a bad idea." Margaret stood at the B and B's front door, having flung it open. Their hostess's eyes danced merrily. "I'm teasing. If I were getting married at the stroke of midnight on Christmas Day I'd feel romantic, too."

Stef slipped away from him, sending him a flirty little smile before wrapping her arm in Margaret's. They walked inside, Stef and Margaret chattering about the ceremony, Emmett hanging back. Margaret's son, the officiant of the wedding, stood in the foyer eating a piece of pie. He put his fork down to shake Emmett's hand.

Emmett listened with half an ear as Lyle discussed the upcoming ceremony, but his attention was on Stefanie. She was wringing her fingers like she was the one with a case of the nerves. He could understand why. She'd probably been planning her future wedding day since she was a young girl, and he hazarded the very safe guess that it didn't involve marrying a man like him. She'd been stoic about their nuptials so far. This was the first time he'd seen her jittery.

A cocky part of him wanted to believe that it wasn't their wedding that had knocked her off-kilter, but the kiss. It sure as hell had short-circuited his brain.

Sliding a stray lock of blond hair behind her ear,

she stole a quick look at him, her lashes dipping almost demurely. They'd share another kiss like that soon enough, this time in front of an audience since Margaret had arranged for a few of the B and B guests to be in attendance for the ceremony.

"I also made a cake." Margaret waved when Stefanie protested that she didn't have to do that, and argued, "It was my pleasure. Now, you two go upstairs and change. When you hear the music, you come on in and we'll start... Unless you had a more formal entrance in mind?"

"No..." Stefanie's eyes flashed to Emmett's like she was checking in with him. He agreed with a subtle head shake. "We want to keep it simple."

At the stairs, she gripped the banister, and he took her other hand, gently weaving his fingers with hers as they ascended the staircase. He only let her go to unlock their room and usher her in.

"Do you want to change in here or the bathroom?" she asked, taking the bagged dress from the closet and tossing it onto the bed. "Or should we adhere to the notion that it's bad luck if you see me in the dress before the wedding?"

She wasn't asking for reassurance. The expression on her face was sheer determination. No longer jittery, she was a woman on a mission.

"I think the concept of bad luck is bullshit."

"Doesn't buy into the concepts of Christmas miracles or true love or bad luck. Got it."

"I didn't say anything about love." He might be incomplete, his heart less than whole, but he'd seen plenty of evidence that true love exists. Chase and

Miriam. Zach and Penelope. Even Stef's parents, Rider and Elle. Just because it wasn't in the cards for Emmett didn't mean it wasn't real. "But you're right on the other two."

She unzipped the garment bag, revealing a sheath of white. He fought the urge to turn his back. To give her privacy or to keep himself in suspense, he wasn't sure which.

"I find it hard to believe you'd agree to marry me out of obligation if you thought your Mrs. Right was out there."

"I agreed to marry you because you made a good case for me to do so. Also, it's terrifying to think of some poor woman tied to me for life."

"That's an awful thing to say to your fiancée!" Her tone was teasing, and so was the feisty twinkle in her eyes.

"My *fiancée* was smart enough to include an escape hatch. You'll be done with me in a few months' time."

Which was best for all parties involved. He could give her what she needed in this moment—a husband—but couldn't give her the forever kind of love she deserved.

He tipped her chin, tempted to kiss her again to feel her lips soften beneath his. He liked the way she'd melted against him earlier; liked the heated way she looked at him now.

"I'll change first and meet you downstairs. Do you need help with the dress?"

"I've got it."

"Is it bad luck to kiss my bride before the wedding if she's not in her wedding dress?"

"I don't think so." She gripped his coat with both

hands and tugged him closer. "Kisses are usually good luck."

"Good luck," he said as he lowered his mouth to hers, "I believe in."

Eleven

Her husband-to-be was ready in minutes, dressed in dark slacks and a white shirt, with a tie he'd purchased in town. At her request, he'd tried on a few suits at the store, but after unsuccessfully wedging his wide shoulders into three ill-fitting jackets, she'd given him a pass.

Even so, he looked *really* good in the cheery red tie that arrowed down his torso and pointed at the thick leather belt. Good enough that she'd given that tie a yank and brought his lips to hers for another kiss.

How they'd return to this room as husband and wife and keep their hands off each other was beyond her. It was also a prospect that was becoming less and less desirable. They hadn't talked about how they'd proceed, but a loveless *and* celibate marriage seemed unfair, unpleasant at best.

She had no doubt Emmett would be able to compartmentalize sex apart from love and marriage, but could she? In theory it sounded easy, but in practice…

Sex muddied the mind and blurred lines. And whenever a past relationship inevitably met its demise, love had been unmasked to reveal its true identity: infatuation.

Love had been an elusive beast for Stef so far. It was one of the reasons she was sure that an arranged marriage with Emmett would work. How could two people who hated each other fall for each other? But the kisses they'd shared so far were proof that he had a bigger effect on her than she'd previously acknowledged.

A *physical* effect.

While she didn't have a problem with attraction, being attracted to him was foreign. And like any other unfamiliar circumstance, she was both excited and nervous to explore. Could they proceed without getting carried away? She wasn't sure. Even the most carefully managed campfire had the potential to spread.

A soft rap on her door brought her out of her ponderings. Margaret's muffled voice announced, "Do you need help with anything, dear?"

When Stefanie opened the door Margaret cupped her mouth with her hands, the older woman's eyes welling with tears.

"Oh, you're a vision!"

"Thank you." Stef turned to admire her dress in the full-length mirror standing in the corner of the room. The sheath dress featured a lacy pattern over the bodice and slim skirt. The halter neckline was supported by thin spaghetti straps that ran over her shoulder blades, fastening at the middle of her back. There was a cutout showing a slice of her lower back. It was sexy but simple—exactly her taste.

"I brought you this, but you don't have to wear it if you don't want to." From behind her back, Margaret produced a hair clip studded with white baby's breath, green leaves and poinsettia petals. "Is it too much?"

"Not at all." Stefanie stroked the petals of the delicate live bouquet. "It's beautiful."

"I made it." Margaret pointed at the greenery. "That's mistletoe. We had extra."

Stef chuckled. To new Christmas memories indeed.

She turned around and Margaret fastened the flowers in place at the back of Stefanie's updo.

"I have your bouquet downstairs waiting for you. My, does your man look handsome."

"Yes, he has that way about him. Does he also look nervous?"

"My son poured him a few inches of bourbon and joined him in a prewedding toast. Lyle says that it's common practice whenever he officiates a ceremony. But to answer your question, no. Emmett doesn't seem nervous. More…excited. Like he's anticipating seeing you. You're going to knock him out cold."

"Maybe I overshot it." Stefanie swept her hands down her sleek skirt. "My goal was simply to keep him at the ceremony until the end."

"Don't worry about that. I'll lock the front door." Margaret elbowed Stef's arm playfully. "Want me to walk down with you? I'll situate the train of your dress and then run downstairs and out of the way."

At the staircase, Margaret took up a length of the dress's skirt and spread it behind her. Stef rested her hand on the railing to keep from tumbling face-first into her own wedding. Her heart pounded mercilessly with each step she took, her mind on her family and how they were going to absolutely freak out when they learned she'd done this without them.

"Miles!" Margaret called from the top of the stairs.

"Your photographer," she whispered to Stefanie. "I'll step out of your shot."

Margaret fluffed Stefanie's dress once more before a thin man with a thick dark mustache stepped around the corner. He lifted his camera, and Stef did her best to hide her thoughts about her family and focus on the present. She smiled as she had for years of family portraits and interviews and a zillion Ferguson Oil events. She was schooled in how to smile with her eyes and position her face for the most flattering angle. As a flash lit the room, she carefully walked down the stairs as classic Christmas carols played in the living room.

Five steps from the bottom, though, her smile faltered, the photographer and guests and background music forgotten. Emmett had been en route to the living room but didn't make it all the way in. He stopped, frozen solid, his mouth dropped open in a gentle gape. Blue-gray eyes scanned her from head to toe, heating when they returned to meet hers.

Margaret tutted and took his arm, practically dragging him into the living room, but not before Emmett's lips curved and he threw Stefanie a sexy, devil-may-care wink over his shoulder.

From his position next to the minister, Emmett swallowed past a dry throat and rubbed together sweaty palms. He'd fooled himself into believing that standing in as a groom would be the same as serving as a groomsman…not that he'd done that before, either. But he'd *attended* weddings before, so he knew the routine.

Watching Stefanie walk toward him in a long white dress was nothing like watching another bride make her way to her groom—mostly because this time, the groom was *him*.

"You've got this," Margaret's son, Lyle, assured him under his breath. He dipped his chin and opened his Bible, and Emmett felt a wobble in his knees that made him wonder how many grooms bit the dust before the vows started.

If what he was feeling were nerves, that'd be not only normal, but expected. But it wasn't nerves that he was struggling with. It was responsibility.

Emmett didn't take his responsibility for others lightly, including this trip with Stefanie. He'd mistakenly assumed that his responsibility was untangling her from Blake by marrying him herself. That the act of saying "I do" would be the end of it.

Wrong.

Stefanie, a red smile on her mouth, her blond hair wound softly at the back of her head, a bouquet of red poinsettias offsetting the stark white of her dress, had made him feel another sort of responsibility for her. He was overcome with the notion of becoming a husband.

Her husband.

Right here. Right now. In front of God and witnesses. And there was nothing mild about that commitment.

In the same way he worked hard to assure himself he earned every dollar he was paid, he wasn't going to marry Stefanie halfway. No matter how they'd originally thought this would go, for him, the ceremony was real. In every way.

Stefanie came to a stop in front of him and sureness rang through him, resonating like a church bell. He wouldn't enter into this commitment lightly. He would give himself to her—as much as he was able—for as long as this marriage lasted.

Margaret stepped in to take Stefanie's bouquet and Lyle instructed Emmett to hold Stefanie's hands.

He did as he was asked, clasping his bride's fingers with his own and meeting her gaze. He nearly sailed off into her aquamarine eyes.

Vows were repeated.

Rings were exchanged.

Her soft "I do" socked him like a punch to the gut.

"What God has joined together, let no one separate." Lyle closed his Bible. "You may now kiss your bride."

Emmett leaned in and pressed his lips to Stefanie's for what was supposed to be a brief kiss. It didn't stay that way. Moving his mouth on hers now that they were married came with a proprietary feeling, giving their union meaning beyond the agreement they'd made. Every pass of his lips over hers was him claiming her as his.

When the kiss ended, their small audience applauded.

His bride's eyes twinkled like the white lights draped over every surface in the room, her beautiful form silhouetted against a white-and-gold Christmas tree. He itched to haul her over his shoulder and take her upstairs, wanting nothing more than to continue their kiss and see how far she'd let him take her.

"I'll pour the champagne!" Margaret announced, snapping him out of the fantasy.

"Champagne?" Emmett asked Stef as the guests stood from their chairs.

"For the toast." She swiped his bottom lip with her thumb and explained, "Lipstick."

"I don't want to have a toast. I want to go to bed." His voice was gravel. His body taut with the desire that felt like a physical presence between them. He let that

sentence hang long enough for her eyes to widen. They
went wider when he added, "With you."

So, yeah. She needed that champagne.

Unfortunately, one glass of bubbly wasn't going to
be enough to erase the X-rated vision of Emmett naked.
She didn't know how much longer she could hang out
at this party before hauling her husband upstairs and
stripping his clothes off.

Alarming, that thought. She'd known Emmett for
years and had never once pictured him naked. Pictured him kissing her. Pictured him as her husband.
And yet here they were. Kissing. Married. And about
to be *very* naked.

"Congratulations, Mrs. Keaton." Anna, a waifish
blonde, was one of the guests at the B and B. She and
her husband, Clay, had been married a little over a year
ago and were here celebrating their first anniversary.

"Thank you."

"The first year is challenging, but in a good way.
Don't believe anyone who tells you the honeymoon is
over if they overhear you arguing."

"Ha. Well. Emmett and I argue a lot, so nothing
new there."

"Even better. The makeup sex is worth it." Anna giggled. Stefanie felt Emmett hovering nearby but wasn't
about to turn to find out if he'd overheard.

Anna stepped away from the crowd a few feet and
beckoned Stef to follow. In the foyer between the staircase and the living room, the other woman leaned close.
"I know who you are," she whispered with a smile. "It
took me a while to place you and then I realized where
I'd seen your photo. The Dallas Duchess."

"Oh?" Stefanie maintained a neutral expression and

tone even as her heart ratcheted up a few notches. That damn blogger.

"What made you decide against a massive wedding in the summer packed with famous guests? Also, I thought you'd be marrying Blake Eastwood. Does your family know you're not?"

Stefanie squirmed at Anna's forwardness and rapid-fire questions.

"I haven't said anything to anyone, and I won't," Anna promised. "But if you don't mind my asking, why are you in Harlington marrying Emmett when that Blake guy said you were his?"

Stef had fielded rumors a million times, but never face-to-face to a nosy woman with zero tact.

"Simple," interrupted a deep, rumbling voice. "Blake's a liar."

Anna started at Emmett's arrival, her mouth gaping. Stef wanted to kiss him for his fantastic timing.

"I need to borrow my bride." He scooped Stefanie into his arms and the small crowd reacted with approving gasps.

"We saved ourselves for the wedding night," he announced. "We're skipping the toast."

Twelve

"Thank you for that," Stefanie said as Emmett set her on her feet in their room. "I have never encountered… What are you doing?"

"Taking off this neck noose." He yanked his tie free and tossed it on the dresser. Then he stalked toward her, standing so close that her dress brushed against his pants. She glanced down and gulped. His *tented* pants. His hand slipped over her back, tickling her bare skin through the cutout in her dress.

"Emmett."

"Tell me to stop. Tell me it doesn't matter that we're married, that you don't want me to touch you."

His words were low and desperate, but his hands never stopped sampling her exposed skin. His fingers trickled up her spine, and his other hand tipped her chin, forcing her to meet his stormy eyes.

"If I kiss your lips again—" he traced her collarbone

with the tip of one finger "—then I'll want to kiss you here next." He clasped her waist with one wide hand. "Then I'll want to kiss you here."

That same hand molded her hip and Stefanie's breathing went shallow.

"And then everywhere," he growled. Only a breath separated them. She felt the barest brush of his lips on hers as her name exited his throat like a plea. "Stef."

She closed that minuscule gap and met his mouth with hers. All she'd wanted to do since he'd kissed her under the mistletoe this evening was touch him more. She melted into him, but where her strength faded, his tripled. His fists wound in the delicate material of her dress as he made good on his promise, moving those drugging kisses down her jawline, past her throat and over her collarbone.

A moan sounded—hers. She hadn't counted on shared attraction as part of this bargain, but it was there in spades. And if he thought she would hold up the stop sign now that they were in their shared room, he was crazy.

Crazy for her, apparently.

She couldn't help smiling at the thought as he unzipped the back of her dress, only to swear when he found a second zipper lower on the skirt.

"You find this funny?" Growly and sort of grumpy. Her scrooge.

"I find you impatient." She fingered the top button of his shirt and unfastened it. "What's your hurry?"

"I want to taste you slowly, but I want you naked *now*."

"I want you the same way, cowboy." She flicked open another button, then one more.

He slipped the straps of her dress off her shoulders,

the rough pads of his fingers causing goose bumps to crop up on her arms. She pushed his shirt open and reached for the undershirt tucked into his pants. The second his belly, and the line of dark hair pointing to his belt buckle, was revealed she flattened her hand over his abs.

He sucked in a sharp breath, his chest expanding impressively. She ran both hands up his torso and cupped his pectorals, the whorls of hair on his chest tickling her palms.

"Damn," she muttered, overcome by the sheer brawniness of him. "You're so big."

"You ain't seen nothin' yet." He stole her breath with another deep kiss, slipping her dress past her hips and leaving her standing in her bra and panties. "What's this?" A deep laugh transformed his face. He looped a finger in the white lace garter belt and snapped the elastic, lightly stinging her thigh.

"Tradition," she said on the end of a gasp.

"Damn," he concluded before kissing her again.

Her fingers fumbled with his belt, her mind on the way he'd looked the first time she'd laid eyes on him in boxer briefs. *Substantial.* But rather than be intimidating, everything about his size only served to make her feel safe.

"I won't break," she assured him when he loosened his hold on her.

"I won't let you."

He ran the flat of his palm between her breasts and pulled the cups away, freeing her. When he dipped his head to suck a nipple onto his tongue, she grabbed his head both to encourage him and to keep from slipping off the edge of the earth. He repeated the favor on the other breast and then her bra was gone, swept away while sparks shimmered over her sensitized skin.

He dipped one thick finger past the edge of her lace panties and brushed her sex with his knuckle. She gasped, damp and ready for him, and they'd only just begun.

"Merry Christmas to me," he said before tucking both hands into the back of her panties and sliding them down her legs. On his knees in front of her, he took a long look at her. She admired the heat in his eyes, the open white shirt and exposed shoulders. His unbuckled belt.

Him on his knees before her.

"I like you here." She raked her hand through his short hair.

His mouth curved with a devilish tilt. "Worshipping you?"

She nodded.

"Bet you're used to that."

"Hardly." The men she'd shared a bed with in her past hadn't been particularly…noteworthy. She liked sex and pleasure, and didn't mind giving as well as receiving, but she'd never use the word *worship* to describe a past interaction. "I can't say I've experienced that."

"A first. Then allow me to worship you." He leaned closer, his warm breath coasting over the scant stripe of hair on her sex. "My *queen*."

Oh yes. That was working for her. Her face warmed, her thighs pressing together in anticipation of the delicious feel of his tongue on her.

He didn't make her wait, slicking her center so slowly her legs shook.

He encouraged her to sit on the bed. Then he was on

his feet, ripping off his shirts and dropping his pants. The bulge in his boxers was as impressive as the rest of him, the thick ridge a promise of the inches to come.

He returned to his task, burying his face between her thighs, and delivering blow after blow of pleasure while she twisted on the comforter. He didn't tell her to come, or command her in any way with his words. Ever the strong, silent type, Emmett let his actions speak for him as he laved her mercilessly.

She let go on a cry that filled the room. The orgasm took its time washing over her and he kept his pace steady until her entire body was sex warmed and sated.

He placed a kiss on each of her inner thighs and then drew a line of kisses up her body as he ascended. Over her, he was more hulking than usual, his turgid cock resting heavily on one of her thighs, his lips glistening, his eyes so lust filled they were almost black.

"I have a condom," she told him. "In my suitcase."

He didn't hesitate to cross the room.

"The zipper pocket."

He pulled out a condom, raised an eyebrow and dropped it back into the pocket. She propped up on her elbows to protest.

"What's wrong?" she asked as he knelt in front of his duffel.

"Too small," was all he said. Then he stood and shucked his boxers and she got an eyeful of *exactly* why the condoms she'd purchased were "too small."

"Merry Christmas to *me*," she murmured, reciting his words from earlier.

He grinned, his chest puffing with male pride, and rolled on the protection from his bag. Then he came to her in fluid movements that should've belonged to a much slighter man.

"You okay?"

His face pinched like he was concerned about her answer. Like she should demurely ask if he was sure he would fit or maybe remind him not to hurt her. She'd do no such thing.

She could handle every inch of her husband's gorgeous member. *Gladly.*

"I'm better than okay, Em." She grasped his biceps and encouraged him forward. *"Bring it."*

There was something beautiful about him at the brink of making love to her. He was a sculpted specimen, perfectly hewed to pleasure a woman. The twinkle in his eye was merry, but determination set his powerful jaw.

"You got it, honey."

He lowered his body between her legs, his hard abdomen lying against her softer belly. He notched the tip into her entrance and slid in slowly, watching her with an intensity that suggested he was in far more pain than she.

"I'm fine. Really."

Then he slid in deeper and she was better than fine.

She arched her neck and enjoyed the fullness of that first thrust, the feel of him seated deep while her body adjusted to his girth. Then she opened her eyes and met his, holding tight to his shoulders as he drew away inch by excruciating inch.

He made love to her as he promised. Slowly. Seductively. Already sensitive from his earlier pampering, her next release didn't take long to build.

Emmett's face was crimped in concentration as he unerringly sought and found the spot that would crumble her will to hold out. She wanted his release more than her own, having already taken advantage of his mouth.

She wanted *him* to let go.

She wanted to watch every second of him coming and record it in her memory.

Because that was what this would be. A memory. As he tenderly slid in again, she reminded herself that they were pretending—that they might be swept up in each other tonight, but the end would soon come for both of them.

"Gorgeous," he praised. "Every inch of you. You feel incredible."

She palmed his cheek, the rough scrape of his scruff sending chills over her entire body. He was pretty damned incredible, too, but she wasn't capable of forming words at the moment.

"Close?" he asked.

"Don't worry about me," she breathed.

He laughed, a low rumble she felt in her rib cage. "Not worried, Stef."

"I want you to come first."

"No deal." His smile vanished, his eyes dark and his expression raw. He doubled his efforts, slowing the pace but increasing the intensity. He watched her like a bird of prey eyeing his next meal, not so much as blinking as he soaked in her every reaction.

When he hit the spot he was looking for, her high cry gave her away. His grin cocksure and beautiful, he lowered to his elbows and cupped her face. Pistoning his hips, he plunged into her faster and deeper, holding her close as she came apart at the seams.

This orgasm hit her harder than the first, the shuddering aftermath leading to a very disappointing realization.

Emmett had come with her and she'd missed the entire thing!

"Cheater," she huffed. "I was trying to make you do that."

"You did." He kissed the very tip of her nose.

"My eyes were closed!"

"I know. I watched." He kissed her chin.

It wasn't fair that he was the one getting the best show. The next time they did this, she'd be sure not to let him take over.

He slipped free of her warmth and she watched his ass as he padded into the attached bathroom. She considered what a dangerous thought it was to decide she'd have sex with her husband again, but she dismissed the concern just as quickly.

She wouldn't let him have the last word, no way. She was going to weaken his knees and melt his muscles at least once before they wrapped up this marriage.

Thirteen

It wasn't Emmett's first Christmas dinner with the Fergusons—far from it. They'd been taking him in as a stray since he'd become friends with Chase. It was almost humorous that he was as comfortable in Rider and Elle's massive mansion as he was in his own apartment, but he supposed he owed most of the credit to the company.

The Fergusons were billionaires—they made more money than Emmett could fathom even though he'd managed to accrue plenty of wealth for himself—but they were also down-to-earth and, at their core, a family.

So when he walked in with Stefanie fresh off the drive home from Harlington, he knew that the unease he felt had nothing to do with Christmas day with her family and everything to do with the fact that he'd married Zach and Chase's sister—Rider and Elle's daughter—and none of them knew it yet.

During the trip back, Stef had mentioned she wasn't going to share wedding pictures online until she broke the news to her family in person, and Emmett had agreed.

Sort of.

He'd suggested she call her siblings and parents and break it to them one by one. Stef had made the astute observation that one of them could tell the others before she did and then she wouldn't be in control of the spin.

Fair enough.

After a quick stop at her apartment to pack her family's gifts, they'd arrived at the elder Fergusons' estate at six o'clock on the nose. He shut off the engine and eyed the front door.

"We're late."

"It's your fault." She slid him a foxy smile that caused him to shift in his seat.

He remembered exactly why it was his fault. He'd been the one to wake her by dipping his head between her thighs. After exquisite morning sex, he'd gone downstairs and fetched breakfast, turned on the television and refused to leave bed until they'd had at least two cups of coffee and a stack of waffles apiece.

He hadn't wanted the morning to end for fear that reality would creep in like some reverse tale of Cinderella. As if, at the strike of noon, he'd be revealed as a servant rather than a prince.

A fraud, unworthy of her hand.

Stupid. But he'd lingered in that room nonetheless.

"Besides, I sent a text to Chase letting him know we'd be late so if he didn't pass that on, it's his fault." She bit her lip as Emmett shut off the car. "How angry with me do you think they're going to be?"

He couldn't keep from touching her, his thumb

stroking her chin with affection. "They'll be pissed at me, not you."

"Don't be so sure. I'm the baby."

"Yes, but you're not *a* baby. You're a grown woman with an incredibly sharp mind and a generous heart. I'll take the brunt of the blame."

She grabbed his hand and tugged him forward, kissing him solidly. He was tempted to pull her into his lap and fog up the windshield before they went in.

It was like the floodgates had opened since that first kiss. Every time he'd touched her since, he couldn't get enough. It awed and amazed him how powerful her pull over him was; how he'd ignored—or maybe *denied* was a better word—that pull until now.

She rested her top teeth on her bottom lip as she took in her parents' house. "Here goes nothing."

They climbed from his SUV, piled his arms and hers with wrapped boxes and then went inside to face the Ferguson firing squad.

"How was she?" Chase pulled Emmett aside to ask.

The presents had been stacked beneath the tree—well, *around*. There wasn't any more room beneath the tree. Dinner had been postponed thirty minutes. As a result, Chase had a few inches of scotch in a glass and had taken it upon himself to check up on Stefanie with his right-hand guy.

Emmett reminded himself that his best friend slash employer had no idea that Emmett was in bed with her that very morning and answered accordingly.

"Smooth sailing."

"Good." Chase's intense glare lessened. "Merry Christmas."

"Merry Christmas." From an inside coat pocket,

Emmett extracted an envelope and handed it over. "It's a museum membership for the year. I figured that'd be better than a jam-of-the-month club."

"You didn't have to—" Chase cut himself off. "Thank you, Em."

Emmett nodded his appreciation at Chase's acceptance and then deposited the other envelopes for Zach and Pen, Rider and Elle, and Stefanie under the tree. He knew none of them needed anything Emmett could provide, but he would never crash their Christmas empty-handed.

He kissed Elle's cheek when she walked in, a glass of champagne in hand. "Sorry we're late."

"I like eating late," Miriam, Chase's fiancée, said. She had no problem taking Emmett's side, especially if it meant disagreeing with Elle. Those two had a past patchier than the quilt on the B and B bed that Emmett and Stefanie had shared.

"I alerted the kitchen staff to keep everything warm since my daughter was going to show up whenever she pleased."

Stefanie's eyelids narrowed with determination. When her mouth opened, Emmett interjected.

"It's my fault. I slept in. Late Christmas Eve celebration."

"How was San Antonio?" Elle asked.

"About that… I have an announcement to make before dinner," Stef said, clearly uninterested in exchanging niceties. "Can you grab Daddy?"

"I'm here. I'm here." Rider stepped into the room with a martini in hand. "Emmett, drink?"

"I'd better."

He took one more glance around the room at Rider in a jacket and tie, Elle in a glittery black dress, Stefanie in a pink dress with lace sleeves. Zach and Pen walked in next, a sleeping Olivia on Zach's hip—all of them dressed to the nines, as well. Chase wore his usual suit and tie, and Miriam was in a green velvet dress. Emmett was in his standard security garb: black slacks, white shirt.

One of these doesn't belong.

As soon as Stefanie broke their news, that fact would become more apparent.

Emmett helped himself to scotch from the bar cart and Stefanie crossed the room to stand next to him. He meant to sip, but when she wove her fingers with his, he downed his scotch in one long, burning swallow before setting the glass on the cart.

"Emmett and I didn't go to San Antonio. We were in Harlington, a small town outside San Antonio where I hosted a dinner for families who can't afford their own Christmas celebrations."

Like mine, he thought numbly.

"Harlington?" Elle said, barely above a whisper, her eyes homed in on Stef and Emmett's linked hands.

"Also, while we were there, Emmett and I were married."

"Oh my God." That was Penelope. She'd been the one to suggest Stefanie get married to extract herself from the Blake situation. Emmett could tell by her reaction that she hadn't meant for Stef to take her suggestion to heart…and she sure as hell hadn't expected Emmett to take Stef up on it.

"Married." Chase spoke next, his tone lethal with disapproval. Miriam stood at his side, her lips pursed as if she was deciding how to process the news herself.

Other than those two comments, no one said a word. Though Zach's hardened jaw suggested he might have reacted if his two-year-old daughter weren't sleeping in his arms.

"We've been in denial about our attraction for quite some time," Stef started.

"This is about Blake," Chase said, not buying it for a second. "You did this to distract from the rumors about you and Blake. And Emmett agreed because you railroaded him into it."

"I did not!" But to Emmett, his wife's tone sounded like an admission of guilt.

"Stefanie." Pen stepped closer, shaking her head. "I didn't mean for—"

"It's not true," Stefanie continued lying. "That may seem like a convenient explanation, but Emmett and I are in love. It's Christmas and we were swept away and—"

"You were married without your family." Elle's voice was both hurt and hard at the same time. "You married Emmett without the approval of your father? Without any of us in attendance?" Her burning gaze hit Emmett next. "We invited you into this family years ago, believing we could trust you, and this is how you repay us?"

"That's on me," Chase said. "I was the one who trusted him to watch over my sister. Which is it, Emmett? Are you in love with her or are you helping her through this Blake debacle to repair the damage done to her reputation and my campaign?"

Stefanie opened her mouth to speak, but Chase held up a hand to stave her off.

"Emmett?" Chase pressed, daring him to lie. Which he wouldn't do.

"We're not in love, but we are attracted to each other," Emmett said. He wouldn't lie to this family. And he wouldn't lie to Stefanie. "The marriage works on both fronts. We can explore our attraction, and Blake no longer has a leg to stand on."

Rider was a wall of displeasure, his face creased, his martini glass empty. He glared at Emmett for a long beat before jerking his eyes to his daughter.

"How long are you planning to carry on with this farce?" Rider asked her.

"It's not a farce, Daddy. We're *really* married. I have the license in the car. I have photos. I'm sharing them on social media later. I wanted to tell you all in person." She let go of Emmett's hand to pull out her phone. She handed it to Penelope, who swiped through the pictures while Zach and Chase looked over her shoulder.

"You continue to embroil this family in scandal," Elle said, her chin trembling with anger. "First you slept with Chase's opponent, and then you marry Emmett without so much as one second's notice to us? And what's with your running off to feed the poor?"

How Elle had said that and made it sound like Stef had run off to join an escort service Emmett couldn't understand.

"It's a noble cause," Stef said. "Some families can't afford presents or a family dinner. I was able to provide a filling meal, a beautiful venue and wrapped gifts for their children."

"Did you vet these people? What if they were addicted to drugs or alcohol? What if they were lying or simply overbudgeted themselves?"

"They were families in need of kindness during a difficult holiday season," Emmett said, unable to keep silent any longer. It was as close as he had ever come to snapping at the matriarch of the Ferguson clan. "Your daughter has a beautiful, giving heart. I saw the tears in the eyes of parents in attendance. She provided a service they needed badly."

He glanced down to see his wife's brows bent with gratitude. She stepped closer and he wrapped a protective arm around her while he spoke.

"Not everyone has the luxury of silver spoons," he continued. "It's a testament to Stefanie's character— and yours—that she would think of people who don't have what she's always had. Your daughter's also a grown woman and you should respect her choices, even if you don't approve of our marriage."

Or me, he mentally added.

Elle had probably pictured her daughter marrying someone well-bred and brought up in the same kind of luxury as Stef was accustomed. Not a man who was an underling to her eldest son.

"I know what I'm doing." Stefanie rested her hand on Emmett's waist as she snuggled closer to him. "Emmett wasn't railroaded." She sent a scathing glare over her shoulder at Chase. Next, she pegged Pen with a gaze, though it was a softer one than the one she reserved for her brother. "And your suggestion may have planted the seed, but it was my idea to propose to Emmett. I know he'd never hurt me. And our attraction is real."

Zach's mouth turned down like he'd tasted sour milk.

"You married some random woman in Vegas and told no one," Stefanie pointed out to him. "And then you two—" her gesture included both Pen and Zach "—pretended to be engaged when you weren't." She went after Chase next. "And you and Miriam were splashed all over the Dallas Duchess blog before any of us knew you were reunited."

She let go of Emmett to stand in the circle of her family and address them.

"I'm my own person, like Zach. Like Chase. Like Emmett. Just because I'm your youngest child," she said, spinning to peg her father with a stern glare, "doesn't mean I'm incapable of making decisions without your approval."

She took her parents' hands with her own. "I love you both, but this had nothing to do with you."

"Marriage is about love," Elle argued. "Not arrangement."

Penelope regarded her shoes. Zach even managed to look sheepish.

"I think it's wonderful." Every head snapped around to Miriam, who'd linked her arm around Chase's. The mayor looked like an emotionless Easter Island statue, but at least he wasn't fuming any longer.

"And married on Christmas?" Miriam smiled. "It's romantic. This calls for a celebration."

Stef smiled back at her future sister-in-law and mouthed the words *thank you*.

"Sometimes things happen out of order and that's okay. That's life." Miriam shrugged before peering up at Chase. "Right, honey?"

Then and only then did Chase's rock-hard facade chip. He gazed down at his fiancée both tenderly and lovingly. "Right."

Stef faced Zach and Pen next. "Right?"

Zach, his daughter a physical reminder that things definitely had happened out of order for Penelope and him, managed a reluctant "Right."

"Okay then. Now that we have that out of the way, let's eat."

Stefanie took Emmett's hand and pulled him toward the dining room. He followed, feeling the entire Ferguson clan's eyes on his back.

Fourteen

The silence at the dinner table was deafening and would lead to a gift exchange that would likely be less merry and bright than it was awkward and stilted.

But Stefanie refused to shoulder the woe of "ruining Christmas." She'd meant what she said about being her own person—about making her own decisions.

She was certain she'd won over Penelope and Miriam, and Zach had seemed less concerned when he'd learned his wife was indirectly responsible.

Chase was another matter.

Stef had always been closest with her oldest brother. She'd been gung ho about her plan originally, but sitting across from him had her doubting herself a little.

The place cards had been rearranged to seat Emmett next to Stefanie per her mother's request—the woman was nothing if not formal. *A husband and wife always sit together*, she'd declared primly.

"Will you change your name?" Pen asked.

"No need for that," Elle interjected, aghast.

"No," Stef answered. She'd rather not agree with her mother, but Elle was right. If Stefanie changed her name legally, she'd only have to change it back.

To her left, Emmett dug into his dinner, uninterested, or unwilling, to participate in this conversation.

"You should." Pen spooned a bite of food into Olivia's mouth.

"Hyphenating is popular. It's what I'm planning on doing," said Miriam.

"Mimi." That was Chase, who sounded equal parts shocked and perturbed.

Miriam patted his arm and promised they'd discuss it later.

"When I announce your marriage to family and friends, I'll simply explain you don't have the same last name as your husband." Elle hadn't touched her dinner, but instead lifted her martini glass. "It's a modern marriage, after all."

"She's not a Keaton," Emmett said. "She's nothing like a Keaton."

"She's a Keaton now," Rider boomed, startling the table into silence. "You took my daughter's hand. You won't shirk your responsibilities as her husband. No matter what you believed when you said 'I do,' you said it. You will honor it."

Adrenaline prickled her fingers as Stef watched the stare down between her father and her husband. Emmett's jaw was granite, and her father's eyes two lumps of black coal. They broke their staring contest when Emmett spoke.

"Yes, sir."

"Will you move in together?" Pen asked. Stef could

practically hear the gears turning about how to spin this announcement to the public. "Your place or his?"

"Mine," Emmett and Stefanie answered simultaneously.

"I'm not moving into your apartment," he stated.

"I have everything I need at my apartment," Stef said. "Your belongings fit into a gym bag. Plus, my home is decorated and my Christmas tree is up and my kitchen is stocked. It makes more sense to live there."

"Why don't you try staying with Emmett tonight? You might like it there," Pen suggested. Stef knew her sister-in-law was only being practical, and possibly trying to end the argument before it started, but Rider and Chase both shifted in their seats, uncomfortable with the idea of Stef going home with Emmett, whether they were married or not.

"I have an idea," Stefanie announced. "Why don't we table this discussion for, oh, *eternity*? And then we can eat Christmas dinner and open gifts in peace."

"What is it about family that is particularly exhausting over the holidays?" Stefanie asked rhetorically as she sagged in the passenger seat of Emmett's SUV. Realizing belatedly that he didn't have a family to deal with over the holidays, she added, "Sorry about that."

"Don't be." He drove in silence, the dashboard's blue lights glowing against his firm mouth. "I understand."

After a gap of silence, she asked, "Do you feel like I roped you into marrying me?"

"Yes."

She winced.

"And I'd do it again." He grasped her hand, giving it a brief squeeze before returning his palm to the steering wheel. "We have something here. It might not be till death do us part, but it's something."

She didn't know what to say to that so instead she said, "It was kind of you to buy for me."

"I buy for you every year."

"Yes, but this year felt…weirder." He'd given her tickets to the fanciest New Year's Eve ball in Dallas, and she had no idea how he'd scored them. Even as Dallas's youngest female billionaire, she hadn't yet managed a coveted invite. "How'd you land two tickets to Sonia Osborne's Sparkle & Shine gala? I've wanted to go for years."

"I know." Those two words were the most touching of the evening.

Who knew Emmett had paid attention to what she wanted or cared about?

He turned into a complex with modern, cozy town houses. Gray siding, white windowsills, charcoal-black roofs. When he turned right onto a street charmingly named Lamplight, she noticed Christmas lights strung on every house but one. And that was the driveway he pulled into and waited patiently for the garage door to raise.

The garage was tidy and organized. One set of metal shelves stood on the right side by an entry door, and on it were rows of black milk crates where he stashed his garage-wares.

"This is it." He shut off the engine. "I'll grab the bags. Go on in."

Since it was cold outside and he offered, she let him do his husbandly duty and entered in through the kitchen. The light was already on, so no there was need to find the switch.

The interior was as manly as the man she'd married

with its dark floors, polished wood, a white ceiling striped with thick exposed beams. Edison lights dangled over a stainless steel countertop, flanked by black cabinetry. She stepped down three stairs that led to a sunken room and flipped on one switch, then another, illuminating a wide-open living room and tall windows, leading to a slatted staircase and a second floor.

If not for the warm lights, Emmett's brown-and-gray town house would closely resemble a nuclear bunker.

"He's all set up in the—oh… Hello."

Stefanie spun around to face the stairs and met eyes with a tall, curvy brunette. Her medium-length hair was straight and sassy, her breasts bursting from a plum-colored V-neck sweater. Her heeled boots and tight leather leggings made her legs look ten miles long and her wide mouth was painted with berry-colored lipstick. Each detail became more apparent as she glided down the steps and into the living room.

"I was expecting Emmett," the beautiful Amazon purred. "I'm Sunday."

Stefanie blinked, not understanding…well, much of anything at the moment.

She folded her arms, unsure who this strange woman was or why she was in Emmett's house. She didn't recall a tale about him having a sister but found herself silently hoping for a pop-up sibling at the moment.

"And you are?" the other woman asked.

"My wife." Emmett joined them and looped his arm around Stefanie's back. "Stefanie Ferguson, this is Sunday Webber."

"Wife. Wow." A sharp glint lit Sunday's brown eyes. She was surprised, and not in an oh-I'm-so-happy-for-you way.

"And Sunday is your…" Stef started.

"Friend," the other woman supplied, her smile snapping into place. She then addressed Emmett, which Stefanie didn't like at all. "Oscar's set up in your spare bedroom. Litter box, food and a few toys. He's grouchy from having to travel, but he'll come out eventually." She waved a hand. "You know what he's like."

Stef didn't like the familiarity in that statement, either. Or the fact that his "friend" Sunday had a key. At least the mention of a litter box stalled any assumption that there was a child named Oscar upstairs.

"This is still okay, right?" Sunday's gaze flickered from Emmett to Stefanie.

"Yeah. It's been a busy weekend. I forgot about the cat, but it's fine."

Stef had a million questions, but she wasn't going to dispense them with Sunday as an audience.

"I'm off to Denver. Thanks again. I'll pick him up next weekend." She moved to Emmett like she would have normally kissed or hugged him goodbye, when Stefanie wrapped both her arms around his waist. She stopped short of hissing.

Emmett's arm tightened around Stefanie's shoulders as if reassuring her. He nodded his goodbye to Sunday. "Have a safe trip."

"I'll let myself out. Nice to meet you, Emmett's wife."

"Stefanie."

"Ferguson. I know." Sunday let that comment hang and wiggled her perfect heart-shaped ass across the living room and out the front door.

Once she'd left, Stefanie let go of Emmett and lifted her arms in exasperation. "What was that about?"

"I'm going to have a drink," Emmett had the nerve to say. "Can I pour you one?"

"Um. Hello?" She chased him into the kitchen. "Who was that? What's going on?"

"That was Sunday Web—"

"Yes. I know her name. Who is she?"

"She's my ex-girlfriend," he stated simply. "Drink?"

"What's your ex-girlfriend doing in your apartment? Why does she have a key?"

With a sigh, he pulled open a cabinet and extracted two wineglasses. He slid a wine bottle from a curved metal hanger on the wall and showed her the label.

Stefanie shrugged. *That's fine.*

"I gave her a key when we were dating," he said as he worked the corkscrew.

"And were you dating when you married me?"

"No." He spared her a glance after he filled his glass, hovering the neck of the bottle over hers.

Stef nodded. She most definitely needed a glass of wine.

"And you watch her cat?"

"He's funny with strangers."

Her brow scrunched—she could *feel* herself scowling.

"Sunday and I are friends and I promised I'd cat-sit. The end." Emmett handed Stefanie her wineglass. She took a sip, the bright red berry flavors bursting on her tongue. Unfortunately, the color of the wine reminded her of both Sunday's lipstick and her low-cut sweater, so Stef found herself frowning anew.

"As you might recall, I had no plans to marry or date you three days ago."

She crossed her arms, knowing she was being unfair but not caring. He rounded the stainless counter and set his glass next to hers, tipping her chin to address her.

"How do you think I felt when you were photo-

graphed coming out of a hotel room with Blake Eastwood?"

She blinked, stunned. "I don't know," she answered
honestly.

A handful of seconds passed in silence, as if he was
debating whether to continue. Finally, he did.

"If you had any idea what I wanted to do to him
after I found out he'd touched you… After I found out
he'd *used* you… If I didn't value Chase's reputation,
or staying out of prison, I'd have torn Blake to pieces
with my bare hands."

It was wrong for her to luxuriate in the notion that
Emmett was jealous, but she didn't care. She let it sur-
round her like a security blanket. All of her grew warm,
starting with her cheeks.

"You didn't like that I was with Blake," she said,
wrapping her head around his admission.

"No."

"And you wanted to hurt him because he hurt me?"

"I wanted to erase him from this planet because he
hurt you."

She reached up and fingered the open placket of his
shirt, his chest hot to the touch. "I feel the same way
about Sunday Webber. Did you love her?"

"Did you love Blake?"

"Of course not. But you already know that. Answer
me."

"Sunday was… That was a long time ago."

"She's very pretty." Stefanie unbuttoned another of
his shirt buttons, then one more. "And *very* busty."
She pressed a kiss to his chest and he sucked in a deep
breath, palming the back of her head. "Say something."
Stef rested her chin on his chest and peered up at him.

"What do you want me to say?" He looked down at her.

"What would've made you feel better after you found out about me and Blake?"

"If you'd never done it." Emmett's chest rose and fell, his hand in her hair.

"What if I told you that I was lonely, and he was falsely charming. Would that make it better?"

"No."

"What if I told you that if I'd known you were in my future—" she undid his remaining shirt buttons and parted the fabric, sweeping her hands along his broad chest "—I never would have given Blake the time of day."

Emmett struck like a snake, lifting her and depositing her on the countertop. She yipped in surprise, parting her legs for his big body a moment later when he stepped between them. "I'd say I liked that a lot."

"Your turn." She linked her fingers at the back of his neck and waited.

His granite-colored eyes warmed as he cupped her rib cage with both hands. "If I had any clue I'd earn my way into Stefanie Ferguson's bed, I'd have remained celibate until my wedding night."

She gulped. He'd rendered her speechless.

"Even if the wedding night was our only night together, waiting would've been worth it."

She tipped her chin and he didn't hesitate to kiss her. She wrapped her legs around the firm globes of his butt, rubbing her center against the hard-on that now pressed against the fly of his slacks.

"Lucky you," she whispered against his panting mouth. "It's not just one night."

Fifteen

Emmett knew it was exactly what Stefanie had wanted to hear, but at the same time, it hadn't been a line. He'd have forsaken all others and waited for her if it would have guaranteed him even one night with her.

It was a realization that shocked the hell out of him. He was coming to terms with the amount of pent-up attraction for Stef that he'd apparently been disregarding over the years, but he didn't suspect there'd been more to it. And maybe there wasn't. Maybe this was the responsibility he'd promised when he'd said "I do" combined with a hell of a lot of attraction. Maybe the core of what he was realizing was about vows and honor—*loyalty*. Loyalty, he understood.

Stef had nothing to be jealous of where Sunday was concerned. The relationship with his ex-girlfriend had been about companionship. Someone to share dinner or watch movies with. He'd mostly gone to her house, though there at the end, she'd talked him into giving her his key. That'd been the beginning of the end. Sunday asking for the "more" that he knew he was incapable of giving. Yet he'd found a way to give that "more" to Stefanie.

He'd told himself that marrying her was to save Chase's campaign and keep Stefanie safe, but if he were forced to admit the truth, he'd been attracted to her for years. Attraction had been dressed up as concern, but it'd been there all the same. He'd shrouded what he now recognized as jealousy with a cloak of anger.

Now with his lips sealed over hers and the tip of her tongue dancing with his, he knew he'd been both attracted to her and burning with jealousy that she'd been in anyone else's bed but his.

He hadn't understood when she turned an envious shade of green over Sunday. Him being jealous of whomever Stefanie touched was understandable. But Stefanie jealous of another woman who'd touched him?

It was *heady*.

Made him feel powerful.

Made him want to strip her bare and take her right on this countertop.

"My queen," he muttered against her throat when he grazed her pulse point with his lips.

"Mmm, I really do like that," she sighed sweetly in his ear.

"Is it too lowly to screw you here and now?" He slid one palm up her skirt and along one thick, honey-sweet thigh.

"You can screw me wherever you like, Keaton," she said, raising her butt off the counter so he could shimmy her panties down her legs. His sly vixen. "I'm your wife. Not your ruler."

"From what I've come to understand, those are one and the same."

She snatched each side of his shirt and tugged him closer, her breath hot against his parted mouth. "Is that so?"

But she didn't let him answer.

"Your mission this time—" she flicked her tongue out to lick his upper lip, and his balls tightened "—is to come before I do."

He grinned, teeth and all. A low laugh rumbled in his gut. "Sorry, toots. You deliver first. Those are the rules."

"We'll see." She grabbed his crotch and stroked his erection through his pants.

Up. Down. Hard. Fast. Then slow again.

He palmed her hand before he lost his mind. "What the hell do you think you're doing?"

His wife smiled up at him. *"Winning."*

Not on his watch.

He knotted his fraying self-control, snatching her hand and bracing it on the counter behind her back. He mimicked the move with her other hand so that her pert breasts were high and lifted with every breath she took.

Her pupils darkened with want, and his body protested not being touched.

"Is this how you want me? Under your control?" She hoisted one fair eyebrow in challenge. "I prefer things the other way around."

"You deserve the royal treatment."

Her expression softened, some of the determination seeping away. Stefanie wanted to be treated well. Deserved to be treated well.

And he was the man for the job.

He left her on the counter and grabbed a stool, sliding

it across the gray-tiled floor and positioning it in front of her. When he sat, his mouth was perfectly at the junction of her thighs. A wily smile on her lips, she spread her legs and showed him a glimpse of the promised land.

"Keep those hands behind you or else," he warned as he rested first one of her knees and then the other on his shoulders.

"You have five minutes. If you fail, then it's my turn."

"I won't fail." It was a vow he took as seriously as any other. Serving her was at the top of his priority list.

"We'll see," she said, and then he went to work.

"Dammit!" Stefanie breathed through her release, cheeks warm and mouth parted.

Emmett's head rose from her thighs and he swiped his mouth before a smirk plastered itself there and stayed.

"So, you won this time. So what?"

He moved the stool aside while she pushed off the counter. When he turned to find her on her feet, he spun her around and smoothed his hands over her bare ass before pulling her dress up to her waist.

"Not done yet, wife." His voice was gravel filled and her response was a whimper of capitulation.

A drawer to her left was slid open and he extracted a condom.

"Why do you have those in there?" she asked, though she wasn't sure she wanted to know.

He rolled on the protection and stayed silent.

"For Sunday?" Stef peeked over her shoulder.

"Shut up." His breath was hot in her ear as he pressed his erection against her. "Do you want this or not?"

"Yes." She did. More than anything.

"Then *behave*."

A moment later he was filling her, taking his sweet time stroking them both to oblivion. Her challenge, and the searching question about why he kept condoms in the kitchen drawer, was forgotten.

"Together." She reached behind her and wrapped a hand around the back of his neck. "Emmett."

"Yes." He nipped her earlobe and gripped her hips, plunging deep. Pleasure ricocheted through her body as he worked hard to match her pace.

"Now. Now!" She tightened her grip on his neck, vaguely aware of her nails digging into his flesh. And then...

They brought down the house.

Her cries mingled with his, their shouts competing for space in the kitchen. His grip loosened on her hips as his ragged breaths tickled her ear.

"That... Amazing." Those broken words were the only two she was capable of.

"Better" came his argument.

She turned, stood on her toes and pressed a kiss to the center of his lips. "Merry Christmas, Emmett."

A blip of what might be memory shadowed his eyes, but only for a moment. In a blink it was gone and replaced with a tentative smile. "Merry Christmas, Stefanie."

His wife excused herself for a bath. He assured Stefanie the tub was clean—he was a borderline neat freak with a lot of free time on his hands. Once he showed her where the towels were and changed into jogging pants and a loose gray tee, he went back downstairs and refilled his wineglass.

His phone showed texts from employees who were

part of Chase's security team—no emergencies, just updates—and from a few friends wishing him a merry Christmas. They didn't know not to. Stef knew not to, but she'd wished him a merry Christmas, anyway. He'd returned her sentiment, the barbs of his past not digging into his skin as deeply as before.

Could've been the world-class sex that helped with that endeavor.

He sat on the brown leather couch in front of a trunk that served as a coffee table, the exposed brick wall punctuated by a simple gas fireplace. He pressed a button to start it and for the first time considered what his place might look like to Stefanie Ferguson. She loved Christmas and twinkly lights and fluffy, fuzzy decorative pillows. He imagined she equated his place with a morgue for all the personality it had.

"Mowr."

Emmett turned his head to find Oscar, Sunday's twenty-two-pound cat, swaggering into the room after almost tripping down the bottom two steps. Graceful, that cat was not. He was good-looking, though, his bright, round green eyes and uniquely patterned brown and darker brown fur making up for the clumsiness.

"Mowr," Oscar repeated, too masculine to manage a dainty sound like "meow."

"I know," he told the cat. "You're stuck with me for about a week. It sucks, but I promise I won't let you die."

Oscar slowly blinked, sitting at the foot of the stairs and curling his tail around his feet. A tail the cat forgot was there a few seconds later when he stepped on it, yowled and sprinted into the next room.

From his seat on the sofa, Emmett shook his head. How he'd ended up with his ex-girlfriend's cat for the week was simple. She'd asked and he couldn't think of a single reason to say no. He'd spent time with Oscar before and noticed he and the feline had a few things in common. They were both supersize, neither of them into frills, both single and both enjoyed chicken salad.

It wasn't Sunday's or Oscar's fault that Emmett had returned home from his trip *married*, so he couldn't very well kick Oscar out.

The water upstairs shut off and he wondered how long his wife would soak. Wondered if he should join her. He smiled at the rim of his glass at the idea of climbing into the water with her and overflowing the tub. He decided to give her a moment to herself. She deserved a break. He'd been in her space, and then inside her, since they arrived at his house.

His phone rang. He answered it without looking. That ringtone belonged to only one individual in his contact list.

"Hey, boss."

"Give me one good reason why I shouldn't fire your ass," Chase said in greeting.

"I'm better at watching your six than anyone on the planet."

A long beat of silence and then, "You hurt her, Em, you'll hear from me. Decorum, my position as mayor of this city and our friendship won't stop me from beating the shit out of you."

"Understood." He'd never roughhoused with Chase, but Chase was no weakling. He worked out, and while the mayor wasn't as wide as Emmett, he had reach. Emmett imagined if he did hurt Stef, he'd deserve whatever justice her brother doled out.

"Is any of it real? I need to know if she's…serving a purpose for you or if you care about her." Chase's voice was steel, his tone the dangerous hum of a transformer about to blow.

"She's an adult. And I'm not Blake. Give me some credit."

"That wasn't an answer."

"I answer to you at work, not about my personal life."

"Emmett."

"Chase. I've been in your life for a long time. I care about everyone in your family. You shouldn't have any worries as to whether I'd hurt her or not. I value your family more than my own life."

Chase's sigh was weighty. He had to know Emmett was telling the truth. Emmett placed loyalty above all else.

"If the scales start tipping," Chase said, "if you notice that she's beginning to care for you more than you will ever care for her, don't drag her along. Let her go."

Chase didn't need to say more. He was talking about love. He meant if Stef started falling and Emmett wasn't falling for her, that Emmett should let her go.

There was no fairer request than that.

"Promise me." Chase's voice was low. "Or it'll be more than your career on the line. I'll cut you out of my family so fast it'll be like we never knew each other."

Even issuing the threat, Emmett could hear in his friend's voice that it was the last thing Chase wanted to do.

"If it comes to choosing between you and my family—"

"Your family comes first," Emmett said, his heart cracking under the pressure of that realization.

He wasn't family. He wasn't blood. Blood in the Ferguson line mattered more than a friendship that spanned a decade. Hell, he'd been surprised Rider and Elle let him walk out of their home with their only daughter since he'd sullied the Ferguson family tree with a Keaton leaf.

Even though it killed him to say it, Emmett couldn't blame Chase for defending his sister.

"I understand."

Sixteen

Movement drew his attention to the staircase. Stef, wrapped in a thick gray bathrobe that she must have found in the back of his closet, held up the yards of extra material and came down the steps like royalty holding her robes.

My queen.

Her frown was evident, the ends of her blond hair dark and wet.

"I heard the phone ring earlier. Which one of my overprotective family members was it?" She clomped over and sat on the couch next to him; the robe balled up and she tucked her legs under her. "Let me guess. The one you serve like he knighted you."

He didn't respond since she'd guessed right.

"That fire feels nice."

Taking advantage of her nearness, he wrapped an arm around her. He wasn't much of a cuddler, but where

Stefanie was involved he was coming to realize the only place she belonged was in the protection of his arms.

"You don't have a single string of tinsel," she pointed out.

He looked around with her at his utilitarian style, the palette of earthy browns and concrete grays, exposed earth-toned brick walls. The decor was a complete an-tithesis of her style. It was like she'd been sent from a castle to live in a cave with the dragon.

His fingers brushed her shoulder, the thick terry cloth keeping him from her bath-warmed skin.

"You don't have to stay here."

"I didn't mean that." She gave him a playful shove, not picking up on the shadow that'd stretched over his soul. "I understand why you didn't deck the halls."

He felt the weight of her ocean-blue stare on his pro-file. He turned to meet her eyes.

"Where is your dad now?"

"Probably at home. Or at a bar."

"Do you see him much?"

Emmett shook his head.

"Do you want to?"

Another head shake.

"I'm sorry." He could hear the sincerity in her voice.

"Don't be. It is what it is." He touched one of her cheeks with his knuckle.

"Well, you have to admit this is the most unique Christmas you've ever had." She smiled, pleased with her joke. Damn if he couldn't help a small smile of his own.

"Unforgettable," he agreed.

He would never forget her. In the event Stefanie started feeling too much for him—more than he could return—then he would let her go home to her family and exile himself in the process.

Part of him howled in protest, the reverberation of that silent cry shaking him to the core. When it came to letting her go, he didn't have a choice.

He'd do it to protect her. He'd do it *for* her.

He'd do it…even though he didn't want to.

The Dallas Duchess. That slimy wench.

The gossipy blogger had swiped the Tweet Stefanie posted this morning, but rather than offer her congratulations, she'd slapped the wedding picture of Emmett and Stefanie on her website alongside a saucy, tawdry headline.

"Stefanie Ferguson Stoops to Marry the Help."

And lookee here, there was even a comment from Blake the Snake. That flaming pile of dog—

"Refill?" Emmett extended his arm, a cardboard box filled with doughnuts balanced in one big hand.

"One is my limit."

"Wimp." He lifted a perfect sugary ring and ate most of it in one bite, a moan echoing in that barrel chest of his.

"Oh, for goodness' sake." She set aside her iPad and stood to take a doughnut, but he tugged the box away and shoved the rest of his into his mouth. He offered her the box again and she snatched a chocolate-covered one and took a sinful bite. After a few swallows of coffee to chase her sugar buzz, she tried to sag on Emmett's couch. Impossible. The back and sides were hard and flat, not a couch meant for sagging.

"I don't typically indulge in something so decadent," she called out as he carried the box into the kitchen. He returned with a mug of coffee in hand.

"Neither do I." He crossed the room and lifted his wallet off the mantel before shoving it into his black slacks. "To be clear, I'm talking about waking up and making love to you."

Damn. Now that was sweet. She had no idea Emmett could be sweet until she'd married him. She'd convinced herself they hated each other—had told herself for years that he only tolerated her because she was Chase's sister. But that couldn't have been true, could it? He'd slipped into her life—into her *bed*—almost seamlessly.

He bent to kiss her. She tipped her chin to catch that kiss and the meaning behind it.

"Ready?"

"Yes." She stood and grabbed her coat while he fetched his own. "Even though I don't think anyone in the free world should have to go to work until New Year's Day."

But she had an appointment with Penelope that couldn't be missed. She hadn't left herself much of a choice.

Emmett pulled to a stop at Zach and Penelope's home. Pen used to have a shingle hung downtown, but since her daughter was born she'd moved her office to the house and employed a nanny to watch over Olivia during work hours.

Zach stepped outside, on his way to his own office no doubt. He wore a suit and a scowl that was meant for either her husband or Stef herself. Maybe it was meant for both of them.

Emmett put down his window when Zach approached.

"Hey, big brother," she chirped. "Before you dole out any overblown speeches and squarely place yourself in the pot-calling-the-kettle-black category, you should know that Chase beat you to it and I don't care what either of you think."

She blew her brother a kiss, and then grabbed Emmett's shirt collar, pulling him close for a real kiss—one he returned, albeit stiffly. He was glaring when she pulled away, and she was flushed, and suddenly wishing she'd started that smooch at his house instead, where they could continue it in privacy.

Anyway.

Stefanie left Zach and Emmett in the driveway and announced her arrival to Pen quietly in case Olivia was sleeping.

"In here. She's upstairs playing." Penelope appeared in the entryway wearing a slimming white dress and waved Stef into her office. It used to be a formal dining room, but they'd converted it into a modern office with French doors and curtains for privacy. Pen shut the door behind her.

"I'm assuming you saw the blog." Stef sat on the white leather couch.

"Oh yes. I check her site regularly." Pen rolled her eyes. "Tea?"

"Please."

Pen poured two cups from a kettle from a small table behind her desk and rested the delicate china on saucers before joining Stef on the couch.

"How's it going?" Pen sipped her tea.

"Fine."

"How real is this marriage?" Pen tilted her head. "Did you consummate it yet?"

"Penelope!"

"Did you?"

Stefanie lifted her tea both to buy time and to wet her parched throat before admitting, "A few times."

"I am going to say something very unpopular."

"Chase and Zach beat you to it," Stef grumbled.

"I like you two together."

Not what Stef was expecting to hear. Pen drew a hard line when it came to her clients, and she could be as bullheaded as Zach when it came to doing things her way.

"He's always watched you. I didn't think of it before, but now that I'm in the family and I've seen him at a few family functions..." Pen nodded as if envisioning one such function now. "Emmett stays in your orbit."

She sent Penelope an unsure smile. The idea that Stef was newly attracted to Emmett made sense—they'd never spent time together unchaperoned until recently. But what about those times he'd lurked in her periphery, or stepped into her line of vision to scowl...

"I guess I always assumed he was in Chase's orbit."

"Yes, but I think that has to do with you. He knows that staying close to the Fergusons comes with the perk of being close to you."

He'd certainly stayed close by lately. They'd slept in the same bed, had slept together, had shared meals and breakfast and had even given Oscar, the cat, a bath after he darted out the front door and straight into a slushy mud puddle.

But for how long? She'd married him with the stipulation that he could walk away. She doubted he would remain in a marriage that was for show. If he couldn't make it work with the buxom brunette *Sunday*, who he easily stayed friends with, Stef wasn't sure she and Emmett had a chance. They'd never been friends.

"I doubt he's the forever type, so don't get your hopes up," she told her sister-in-law.

Pen let out a *pfft* sound of disagreement and rested her cup and saucer on the glass coffee table.

"What was that for?"

"You are the one who personally pulled Zach's head out of his ass when he and I split. How can you say Emmett has no hope?"

"That's different. Zach's so obviously in love with you."

"And I'm in love with him." Pen's smile was gooey before vanishing altogether. "Are you in love with Emmett?"

"What? No! How?" Penelope wisely remained silent but Stefanie kept protesting. "I can't be in love with him. We've only been married for thirty-two hours."

"Yes, but you've known him for *years*."

"You're making no sense." Stef swept aside the conversation with one hand. For one, it was making her uncomfortable, and two, it was…making her uncomfortable. "Advise me how to behave in public with him. That's what I want to know. That's *all* I want to know."

She didn't want to entertain an idea that her heart might follow where her body led—that she might stumble and fall into a big pile of "I love you." She knew how this ended—Emmett and Stef had constructed the end from the beginning.

But Pen wasn't convinced. "Mmm-hmm."

Well, Stefanie didn't need to convince her. She didn't need to convince anyone of anything. And she certainly didn't need to entertain the notion that happily-ever-after was in store for her and Emmett.

It wasn't.

It was as simple as that.

Seventeen

"Try to look like you're not completely miserable."

Stefanie's arm was looped in Emmett's as she stood at his side at the museum fund-raiser. She'd dragged him to the event, being held at the Dallas Museum of Art in the Renaissance room, but attending the private function had been Penelope's bright idea.

His wife wore her for-the-public expression, an amiable twist of her lips suggesting she had a secret no one knew but her. Meanwhile, his frown was frowning. He wasn't good at faking anything. He hadn't had the practice and, frankly, didn't give a damn what anyone thought.

His arms were straight at his sides, his fists wound into twin hammers. His focus jerked around the room in search of a particular lowlife by the name of Blake Eastwood, who was "scheduled to appear," according to Pen. Personally, Emmett would have liked to find and pummel him into paste.

"Or like you're out for blood," Stef whispered as they walked through a pair of velvet ropes. A security guy in a tux asked for their tickets and Emmett handed them over.

Pen had also arranged for a local photographer to be here to snap photos of Emmett and Stef holding each other close. Bonus if it included a seething, flame-red-faced Blake in the background.

"Breathe."

"I'm not as good at this as you," he said between his teeth. Understatement. Given the choice, he'd rather be in the background five hundred percent of the time and in the foreground never. *Ever.*

Stef walked him to a painting, a huge, wall-size painting of angels and demons and people with knives in their guts and dogs snarling, their teeth bared.

He wasn't sure which of the subjects he identified with most at the moment.

Next to him, his wife pressed close, her breast brushing his arm. She was wearing a short black dress, the slit in the side high enough to expose one creamy thigh when she walked. Her boots were the pair he'd taken note of in Chase's office: knee-high with brass buttons running the length and ending in high, spiked heels.

His attention on her helped his temperament stabilize. She'd had a calming effect on him lately—sleeping with her was probably the dominating factor in that effect. Before he'd taken her to bed, whenever she was around he'd been strung as tight as a string on that angel's harp.

"Keep your eyes on me," she told him. "Pretend I'm the only person in the room."

"I can't." He lowered his voice so they wouldn't be overheard. "I'm trained to notice that the old guy standing by the Renoir is checking out your ass, and a blonde lady is snapping pictures of the whole event in the corner by a painting of a well-endowed woman eating grapes."

"That's our planted photographer. She's legit."

He slid a glance over at the woman again and then back to the old guy. To Stef, he said, "Wasn't Renoir an Impressionist? I feel like that painting's in the wrong room."

Stef grinned. "Impressive, Mr. Keaton."

"I have my moments."

He'd always watched over Stef. She was in his sights because he watched over Chase, and she was an extension of Chase. He'd regarded her like he had any of her family members. Although, that wasn't true, was it? He'd felt a pull toward her that eclipsed standard Ferguson concern. And now his desire to protect her was stronger than it'd ever been—and growing. Those wedding vows weren't only for show. He'd taken them to heart.

She towed him over to a different painting, another he didn't recognize, tucked into a quiet corner that was populated only by them.

"How's this?" she asked.

"Perfect. Let's live here." He took a quick look around to make sure they weren't being watched. When her hand brushed innocently over his crotch, he jerked his attention back to her.

"I'm the only person here."

"If that were true—" he lowered his lips to hover just over hers "—you'd pay for that."

She nuzzled his nose and he caught himself smiling down at her, his arm wrapped around her waist. Something about the way she tipped her head told him she was posing.

"Is it happening *now*?"

"Yes. The woman by the grape painting. Kiss me."

He'd intended to give her a chaste kiss, but chastity where he and Stef were concerned always approached inappropriate. By the time her tongue touched his, he was ready to get the hell out of here.

Her attention moved from him to across the room and she gripped his arm, giving it a hard squeeze. "He's here."

Emmett didn't have to ask who "he" was. Blake, with a small-boned, big-eyed woman on his arm, glided into the place like he owned it. Smarmy bastard. He turned and spotted Stefanie, then Emmett and stopped cold.

Emmett pulled his wife closer.

Mine.

Blake, incapable of taking a hint, excused himself from his date and completed the journey over to where they stood.

"Stefanie." Blake ignored Emmett.

"Blake." She rested her hand on Emmett's torso. Anyone looking on might think she was smoothing his tie, but Emmett knew she was attempting to tamp down his ire. Didn't work. The need to punch Blake's face in still simmered.

"I noticed—" Blake started.

"Get the hell away from her." Emmett was off script, but he didn't care.

Blake's face oozed into a smile. "Relax, Keaton. You've clearly won this round. Though I never dreamed she'd sell herself off to you."

Emmett's arm flinched and Stefanie moved both hands to his forearm. Blake jerked away before sending Stefanie a bemused smile.

"Better keep your dog on a leash, Stef. Is he the best you could do on short notice?" Blake asked. "Some wild animal that can't be taken into public?"

"Better a wild animal than a slithering, slimy reptile." Stef loosened her hold—which she was about to regret. Emmett had enough of this conversation. The condition of Blake's nose relied on his own response.

Blake sneered. "That's not what you said when I took you to bed, unless you mean—"

Emmett shook off Stef's hold and slammed a fist into Blake's face.

"You were warned," Emmett growled.

The other guests gasped and backed away as the blonde with the camera ran forward to catch a pic of the action. She'd snap a good one, too, given that Blake was doubled over, streams of blood running between his fingers. His date cooed over him, but Emmett was done.

He took Stefanie's hand and led her from the event, splitting the crowd like well-dressed bowling pins.

"No matter how hard I try, I can't be upset with you." Stefanie moved the plastic bag filled with ice from Emmett's knuckles to inspect his red fingers. "No scrapes, though. Impressive."

"He has a soft face." Emmett smirked at his own joke. "I'm done with the ice."

She went to the kitchen and dumped it into the sink, returning with a beer for him and a glass of wine for herself.

He accepted the bottle, taking a few long swallows. She watched the column of his neck work as he drank, wanting nothing more than to drag her tongue over his Adam's apple. Never before had she thought of Emmett as "sexy" but now that she saw it, it couldn't be un-seen. She'd been wondering lately how she'd missed it.

His legs were spread, knees wide as he sat on his couch. She had no idea how he could like that rigid piece of furniture. She took the equally uncomfortable chair nearest him.

"Mowr." Oscar padded into the room and she stroked the cat's back. He responded by arching, his tail flicking into the shape of a question mark.

"I like this cat despite him belonging to your ex-girlfriend."

Emmett sighed, evidently not wanting to return to this discussion.

"I suppose we'll see her sooner or later."

"Later," he said. "She extended her trip."

"And stuck you with her cat?" Stef stroked Oscar again and winked her apology.

He wasn't any trouble, really. Even though the day she'd bathed him he'd looked at her like she was per-forming torture as she shampooed the mud from his coat. Oscar had claimed the guest bedroom for himself but trotted into Emmett's bedroom to greet his tempo-rary human caretakers each morning. More often than not, the cat approached her side of the bed and she'd murmur her good morning before walking downstairs to feed him. It wasn't lost on her that this entire setup—the cat, the marriage, her living with Emmett—had an expiration date. Soon she'd be in her own bed, cat-less and Emmett-less. The thought bothered her more than it should.

She didn't even know she liked cats.

Or Emmett, she thought with a soft smile.

"What are you wearing to the Sparkle & Shine gala?"

"Sorry?" His face pinched in confusion.

"The tickets you bought me to the New Year's Eve party. You're accompanying me."

He digested that information for a second. "I didn't picture myself as your date when I secured them."

"Who did you picture as my date?"

"Someone…else."

"Not Blake."

"No." His visage darkened. "Not Blake. But someone…" He appeared to roll a few options around in his head before deciding on his answer. "Not like me."

"Someone who…doesn't work for my family?"

His stare was grave. "Yes."

"Someone—" she rose from her seat on the chair and sat with him on the couch "—who knows how to behave in public?"

She crossed one leg over the other. His eyes ran the length of her boots slowly. She'd noticed him admiring them before.

"You like these?" She pointed a toe.

"Immensely." His fiery gaze locked on hers.

"Who knew attraction was hiding under all this… animosity?" She fiddled with the collar of his shirt. "I always thought you hated me."

He didn't deny it, but he was scowling.

"The way you slid me those glares whenever I came to visit Chase at work. Or whenever you came to my parents' house for a party." She pointed at his face. "Like that. I bet no one believes we're in love."

A tiny needle of sadness pricked her, but she ignored it. Obviously, *she* knew they weren't in love, but that didn't mean she couldn't take advantage of his nearness.

"There's a thin line, my queen." He broke eye contact to lean, his elbows on his knees, his beer dangling between thick fingers. He was so easy to admire. She'd never thought to admire him before. She thought she'd disliked him as much as he disliked her.

Now they liked each other in equal measures. When had that happened? She guessed somewhere between convincing him to enter city hall with her and the moment he insisted on buying the ring and sliding it onto her finger. She blinked, coming to the slow realization that what was between them couldn't be categorized as simply physical. He blew her mind in bed, but he also honored her at every turn. Like tonight, when he'd broken Blake's nose.

Gosh. She really hoped he'd broken it.

Stef had never been treated like gold by a man. By her father and brothers, sure, but never in a romantic relationship. She'd always been willing to have fun and made it clear she wasn't interested in being tied down. Yet here she was. Having fun *and* tied down.

Temporarily tied down. She couldn't forget that part.

Even though during these quiet moments with Emmett, she wished she could.

Eighteen

Thankfully, no photos from the museum surfaced. Penelope made a call to the photographer and paid her generously to bury the photos of Emmett hitting Blake in the nose. The story was officially dead. The Dallas Duchess had posted about "whisperings" that Blake had two black eyes, but she'd been "unable to reach him for comment."

Over the span of what amounted to only a couple of days, Stefanie had made her way from the top of the news feed online to somewhere in the middle. She'd never been so happy to not be "trending."

She set her phone on the counter as Emmett stepped into the kitchen, freshly showered and dressed for work, eyeing her with a primal gaze that reminded her of everything she'd done to him last night—and everything he'd done to her this morning.

Sharing his bed each and every night was much

better than she'd anticipated. And she barely missed her apartment—well, she missed it a little. Mostly the cheery baubles sitting around that made her apartment feel like a home.

There were no baubles in Emmett's town house. It was stocked with necessities. Utilitarian and simple.

"You need a painting or two."

"Why?" His frown was outlined by the light from the open fridge door.

"What do you like?" she asked rather than answered.

"I like *not* to dust superfluous surfaces."

So much for that idea.

Bottle of half-and-half in hand, he moved to the cabinet for a mug.

"We're off the top-ten list of people to talk about in Dallas," she said. "Blake has retreated into a hole in the ground. For now."

"Good. I'll check in with the staff at the mayor's office and make sure the heat's off Chase." Emmett lifted the coffeepot and filled a mug. "In hindsight, he's the one who should've gotten married to salvage his campaign and take the heat off you."

The comment settled into the air like a foul stench.

"Having regrets?" she asked.

"That's the wrong question."

"That's not an answer."

"No. I'm not having regrets. Regret is as useless as worry." He crossed the kitchen and put a kiss on her forehead. "So stop doing it."

Who knew gruff and sweet could coexist in one big, burly package? He continued to surprise her.

"The gala is tomorrow."

"I know."

"I'm going to have to stop by my apartment to dig

through my closet. I've been too preoccupied to shop properly for a dress and now it's too late."

"The tragedy of off-the-rack," he said with a healthy dose of sarcasm.

"It's your fault!" she accused with a grin. "You keep me in bed for longer than I've ever stayed there before."

He set aside his steaming coffee mug to cup her jaw. "That's because there are far more fun things to do with you in my bed than out of it."

See? Sweet.

She savored the feel of his giving and taking mouth, losing herself in the fantasy that this was her life. Their life. That they'd come home each and every day to each other—and to their cat, Oscar—and argue about what to wear to the next social function or what kind of art belonged in their home.

And when he tilted her head to deepen their kiss, she wondered if he wasn't doing the exact same thing—reveling in this moment rather than dealing with reality.

Chase's nod was final but there was an ellipsis in his eyes.

"Spit it out, boss." Emmett shut Chase's office door and crossed to the middle of the room to stand before his best friend, arms folded.

His armor.

"How's it going?" Chase asked, and Emmett lifted an eyebrow at the mild line of questioning.

"Peachy."

"I'm serious."

"The world is my oyster," Emmett responded, his tone flat.

Chase offered a head shake and pinched the bridge of his nose. "God, what a mess."

Whether he was talking about Emmett marrying Stef or about the Blake drama, it was hard to say.

"The heat's off you for the immediate future. Relax in that."

"I assume you're attending the Sparkle & Shine gala with Stefanie tomorrow night?"

There was a segue.

"So I'm told."

"Mimi and I will be there. Sonia Osborne sent me a pair of tickets. Evidently she's a fan of the mayor." He smoothed his tie and lifted his chin. Smugness was a good look on Chase. Emmett preferred it to his best friend threatening to kick him out of the only family he had.

That was the inevitable conclusion, wasn't it? Stefanie poured her entire heart into everything she did— charity Christmas dinners, dressing for events… *marriages*. She was in deep—he could feel it. And the tragedy was that to keep his word to Chase, Emmett would have to eventually walk away. Because he didn't have an "entire heart" to pour into anything— or anyone.

Dread crawled up his spine at the thought of losing it all. *Again.*

"Don't look so downtrodden. It's a party, not a natural disaster," Chase said. "All you have to do is show up, have a few drinks and deliver a New Year's kiss… to my sister."

He tacked on that last bit as if it'd just occurred to him.

"That's taking some getting used to." Chase slid a glance at Emmett, who dropped his arms. "For both of us, I presume."

Despite the hope in his friend's voice, Emmett couldn't agree.

"Stef and I have it down. We're good."

Chase's eye twitched, but his words were encouraging. "I wouldn't want her to be unhappy. Or you."

"All due respect, boss, but she's the important one." Emmett was trained in the art of being unhappy. He could handle it if he had to be that way again.

"Agreed." Chase's desk phone purred at the same time Emmett's cell phone buzzed. "Work calls."

Emmett gripped the doorknob and checked his phone, pausing to read the message and decide what to do about it. Chase's voice faded into the background.

The text lit both Emmett's phone and his brain on fire.

The photo was Stefanie's tall, sexy boots he'd grown so fond of. Toes pointing, a concrete square of sidewalk in the city beneath her feet, that pair of knee-high boots sent his mind straight to the gutter. The following text message blanked out everything else.

How about I wear these tonight? ONLY these.

"Em." Chase's voice crashed into his psyche.

Emmett tucked the phone into his pocket as guiltily as if Stef had sent him a nude selfie instead of a photo of her shoes.

"What?" he snapped.

Chase frowned, phone still against his ear. Oh, right. Work. Chase briefed him on a potential issue and asked that he relay it to the security team. Emmett listened, his mind slowly descending to earth, where it belonged.

With a "No problem, boss," he yanked open Chase's office door and got to work.

* * *

Penelope, a glass of sauvignon blanc in one hand, was all smiles. She'd taken a break from work when Stef called her to catch up. The invite hadn't come because of a PR need, but because Pen was now her sister and Stef hadn't been a very good one. Lately her relationship with her sister-in-law had revolved around Stef screwing up and Pen bailing her out.

Not cool.

"Can I get you ladies anything else?" the waitress, a young brunette, asked.

"Just the check," Penelope said.

"On me," Stefanie interjected. The waitress nodded her understanding and walked away. "I owe you, Penelope. Also..."

She extracted her cell phone, called up the text she'd sent to Emmett before lunch and showed Pen.

Penelope's face was serious for a beat until she figured out that Stef wasn't showing her dirt she'd have to clean up, but a fun little secret she'd told no one about until this very moment.

"I love it." Pen gasped, proud. "I love his response more."

Stef grinned as she reread Emmett's response for the fourteenth time.

Hell yes. That was it. He expressed himself as he normally did: without decorum or silly emoji. Just two words, straight to the point.

"This arrangement is working out between you two."

"It's early. I'm not sure we've passed the will-we-make-it portion of the test yet."

"That's ongoing." Pen waved a hand in dismissal. "Miriam hit the nail on the head the night you announced you two were married. I'm also over everyone trying to do things the 'right' way. Your parents mean well by worrying about you, but you're an adult. You make your own decisions and if they don't accept that, that's on them."

"Right." Stef nodded, feeling vindicated. She'd been trying to prove to them—hell, to everyone—that she was responsible for a while now. "I didn't do this to spite them. I did this for myself. And for Chase."

"What about Emmett's parents? Did they have a kitten when you told them the news?"

"We…didn't tell his dad. And his mother died a long time ago." Sharing any more about his family felt like a betrayal. She trusted Pen implicitly, but it wasn't Stef's story to tell.

"I'm so sorry to hear that. I assumed they weren't close since Emmett shows up at so many Ferguson functions. If you count in years, he's a bigger part of this family than me. Does he plan on reaching out to his father?"

"Not that I know of. It's…complicated." Impossible, really, but who was she to judge?

"Give it time. If it feels like the right move to include his family in your life, you'll know it."

"That's assuming a lot, Pen." Stef reached for her water glass.

"Not too long ago I was on the fast track to building my business into a Fortune 500 company, I'd sworn off men, and I was fairly sure I'd never have children." Pen waggled her wedding band. "Now I'm married to an oil tycoon, raising a daughter and advising the wealthiest family in Dallas."

"Not just advising." Stef reached for Pen's hand and squeezed. "You're family."

Just like Emmett was. Just like he'd always been.

Except where Stefanie was concerned, that bond had taken on a new, more interesting shade. He was at her side, making her see life differently. Helping her see herself differently. She was beginning to wonder if she would've uncovered the stronger side of herself without him.

"I like having you as a sister, Stef." Pen, an only child, smiled, her eyes misting. "It's an honor."

"Same to you. You're the best thing that's ever happened to Zach."

The waitress set the bill on the table, but Pen wasn't finished with her assessment yet.

"I have a feeling Emmett feels the same way about you."

Chills ran the length of Stefanie's arms as she considered that possibility. Could it be that as much as he was unknowingly giving to her, she was also giving to him? Giving him the same sense of family and belonging on a more intimate level than he'd ever experienced? It was heady. It was…scary. Was she ready for something so…life changing?

Pen's smile turned saucy, unaware of Stef's bend of thought. "Have fun in those boots tonight."

"Oh, I will." Stef stabbed her credit card into the black book as she offered the expected response. In truth, Pen's assessment had taken hold. Could there be more to come in Stef's little marriage?

The prospect of more excited her right down to the toes of her sexy boots.

"Hello?" Stef called from Emmett's empty, dark kitchen.

"In here."

She stepped into the living room to find him in front of the fireplace, a beer in hand, a frown on his face.

"Everything all right?" She'd expected to come home to a trail of rose petals leading to the bedroom after his response to her text. Well, maybe not rose petals, but she'd expected him to be at least excited to see her.

"Fine."

From a shopping bag in her hand, she pulled out a bottle of champagne. "I thought we could have a sexy evening. Sexy begins with champagne."

She'd actually thought they'd have a *romantic* evening, but the adjective might be too much for Mr. Emotes Not.

"I have a beer, but thanks."

She sighed her disappointment.

"You look beautiful." He stood and came to her, lowering his mouth for a kiss she accepted. "Can I pour you a glass?"

"No, that's okay. We'll save it for brunch." His stony expression sent an ominous shiver up her spine. "What's wrong?"

"I spoke with Chase today."

"Major mood killer." She slid the champagne back into the bag and set it on the trunk coffee table.

"He doesn't want you to be unhappy." Emmett's expression remained severe. "And neither do I."

"I'm not."

"Are you sure?" He studied her as if asking a deeper question. "Because if you're not...you don't have to stay married to me until your brother is reelected."

She blinked, stunned mainly because she'd begun thinking in the opposite direction. That maybe, if he was open to it, they could remain married awhile longer.

And here Stef had spent the day imagining that Emmett's feelings were deepening for her.

Raw acceptance reflected in his eyes. "I don't want you to leave, but if you're ready to go…it's okay."

"Emmett." She palmed his face. "I don't want to leave."

He exhaled, and to her it sounded as relieved as she felt.

"Besides…" What if they ended up like Penelope and Zach? What if the pretend became real and a happy life followed? Stranger things had happened. "What if we defied odds and made it? What if we stayed married, had great sex and you continued defending my honor at public gatherings?"

"What are you saying?" His expression was tortured, his jaw set.

"It's working. That's what I'm saying." There had been plenty of prognosticating about this marriage— from the bloggers, from the public and from her family. She'd even caught herself wishing for a crystal ball so that she could see what lay ahead. But no one, no matter how vehemently they stated their opinion knew what the future would bring. Emmett and Stef were in charge of that.

She knew her husband on another level than "her brother's friend." Stef and Emmett might not have been outwardly friendly over the years, but their bond was deeper than surface. If it wasn't, there was no way she would've felt comfortable sharing a bed—sharing a life—with him. Not even for show.

And if she descended into the dark, private depths of her soul, she'd admit to feeling a ripple of wanting more. Since her "I do" at the wedding, she'd done more than pretend to have more. She'd *embraced* it. Now that it was shaping up to have potential, and if Emmett didn't want to leave any more than she did, why not explore what they had?

"You can't know it's going to work. Not after a handful of days." He turned away and scrubbed his jaw. Stef couldn't tell if he was more tormented by the idea that they could last, or by the idea that they wouldn't.

Sure, it was scary, but if they faced it together it somehow seemed doable. Scarily doable.

"Plenty of couples implode after *decades* of being together. You think they knew any better than we do?" She pulled his hand from his face and smiled at up him. "You don't have my gut. I trust my gut."

She trailed a finger over his neck and into the open placket of his shirt. He palmed her back, lust replacing some of the pain in his eyes. Stef had the stray thought that she would do almost anything to keep the pain out of his eyes. Including moving this conversation into the bedroom, where they were always on the same page.

She continued trickling her finger over the buttons on his shirt, stopping short of grabbing his belt buckle and demanding he carry her to bed for some naughty, too-fun-for-words sex.

Turned out she didn't have to.

He bent and scooped her into his arms.

"Champagne can wait," he rumbled as he carried her to the stairs. "I have plans for you and these boots."

Nineteen

When Emmett had gifted the Sparkle & Shine gala tickets to Stefanie for Christmas, he'd been a *million* percent sure she wouldn't ask him to attend as her plus-one.

And he'd been a million percent sure that the man who came with her would be someone who knew how to smile for the camera. A clean-cut, refined guy in a suit who would appear affable to any onlookers.

So. Not. Him.

He knotted the strangling bow tie at his neck, his tension rising.

He was aware that he had a responsibility to her and to her family not to take advantage of Stefanie in any way, shape or form. But he was also staunchly aware that the attraction they had for each other wasn't going to evaporate into the ether. They'd been ignoring it before, and even if they signed annulment papers today, there was no denying the hot snap of awareness every time she stepped into his personal space.

He hadn't been able to escape the words Stefanie had said about their marriage before he took her to bed that night.

It's working. That's what I'm saying.

It was working. As long as no one started confusing great sex for something more. Something...deeper.

She wasn't beholden to him. If she wanted to resume her normal life, he wouldn't stand in her way. However, he was beholden to her. Both Stefanie and the Fergusons as a whole.

Emmett was duty bound to the Fergusons and had sworn years ago to protect them at all costs. That was what family was supposed to do—a lesson he'd learned from the Fergusons since his own father had done a piss-poor job of setting an example.

Van Keaton had taught him that when the going got tough you looked out for number one. Forget that your brokenhearted six-year-old son was as unmoored as a ship lost at sea. Forget that you had a responsibility to let family and friends know how to contact you rather than hide behind closed curtains in a shabby apartment in a bad part of town.

His parents' extended families had been distant and scattered, so they fell by the wayside after Emmett's mother died. Not helping was that his grandparents on his mother's side never approved of his mother marrying Van. He was bad news, they'd said. Selfish, they'd argued. By the time Emmett had grown up enough to recognize that they were right, his grandfather had passed and his grandmother was in an Alzheimer's disease facility and didn't know her own name, let alone his.

"Whoa, baby." Stefanie entered the living room via

the stairs, a vision in a sparkling gold gown. The color made her fair skin shimmer, and her hair fell over her shoulders in matching golden curls. "You look hot."

"Took the words out of my mouth."

Emmett had seen Stefanie in a lot of dresses at a lot of fancy parties, but she'd never been more beautiful than she was in this moment.

Because he was her date? Because she was in his house?

Because she's yours, his brain argued.

He stuffed that thought to the back of his head, where it belonged.

She swept over to him and he folded her into his arms. It was as natural as breathing. She *fitted* there.

"Sadly, my boots don't match this dress." She poked the toe of a strappy gold sandal from beneath the long skirt.

"Not complaining." He eyed her gold-painted toenails. "Though I have a newfound appreciation for your boots."

That'd been some sex for the books. Stefanie in knee-high black leather boots straddling him. *Riding him.* Her pert breasts had bounced to the rhythm she set while a sheen of sweat coated her skin as she worked them both into a frenzy.

"Dammit." He adjusted the bulge behind his fly and blew out a tormented breath. His wife *beamed.* "Stop looking so satisfied with yourself."

But he liked when she was satisfied with herself. She should be. And not for making him come—that was simple mechanics. The part that was all Stefanie was the way she'd caused his head to detach from his neck and float into the atmosphere. And when he'd finally come back down to earth, he'd been greeted by her draped over his chest, her fingers playing with his chest hair, her sultry sighs of pleasure in his ear.

She'd absolutely *owned* him in that bedroom. And that was a feat no other woman could claim.

An hour later they stepped into the ballroom where the gala was being held. The ritzy, high-end mansion made Chase's mansion look like a cute starter home by comparison. The color palette was übermodern silver and blue, the theme an aquatic one. Glass room dividers with rivulets of water running down them separated the room into sections and ice sculptures accented every corner. One was shaped like a massive merman, another like a conch shell that doubled as service for a buffet of cocktail shrimp, and there were several other smaller frozen vignettes lit with blue or green lights. Music thumped the speakers and guests stood around high-top tables with bases shaped like seahorses.

"Oh! Champagne. We must." Stefanie was a ball of energy, fitting in at the gala like she'd planned it rather than simply attending as a guest.

Emmett had landed the invitation from Sonia herself after having received a call from her assistant that Sonia was in need of a bodyguard for an event last year. He'd phoned one of the key players off his security team and Doug had picked up the gig, happy for the extra money. Sonia had given two tickets to the event to Doug, who had handed them over to Emmett without a second thought.

"I'm not sure I belong in this crowd," Emmett told his wife.

Understatement. He most *definitely* did not belong in this crowd.

"Don't be silly." She handed him a flute filled with bubbly liquid.

"Your net worth has about a hundred more zeroes than mine."

She rolled her eyes. "We didn't sign a prenup, you know. My income is your income."

"No. It's not." He cupped her elbow, making sure he had her attention. "I'd never take your money, Stefanie."

"So serious all the time."

She took a sip of the champagne, her eyes on the near-barren dance floor lit by wavy, undulating lights meant to look like water. He could've guessed what she was about to ask, but before he could argue she'd divested them of both their glasses.

"Dance with me."

"No."

Her husband had turned obstinacy into an art form.

Sliding her hands into the black jacket and over his crisp white shirt, she tipped her chin, taking in every big, grouchy inch of him. The tuxedo had nearly turned her into mush tonight. On the drive over, she was tempted to untie that bow tie and then palm his crotch while murmuring dirty, fun promises in his ear.

She hadn't, though, and now regret was a heaving, growling beast.

"It's time to admit that you've earned me."

He said nothing, but the storm in his blue-gray eyes said plenty.

She could read his pained expression as clearly as if he held a cue card. She didn't like what she saw. He believed he was beneath not only the people at this party, but Stefanie herself.

Suddenly, she wasn't interested in waiting until they arrived home to have her way with him. She was going to teach him an unforgettable lesson *and* collect what she'd wanted from him since their first night together.

Him. Tumbling over the edge of the orgasm cliff *first*.

"Walk with me." She palmed his forearm. When he resisted, she gripped him tighter. "I promise no dancing."

He walked with her as they meandered away from the crowd.

"No one here is better than anyone else no matter how much they'd like you to think so," she leaned close to say. "No one is above gossip and I've heard it all. Monique's third husband, Samantha's Botox addiction. Terrence's calf implants."

Emmett raised an eyebrow.

"You heard me."

She walked arm in arm with Emmett until they reached a curtained-off section at the back of the room. A thick swath of semisheer fabric was lit by a wall of white twinkle lights but she couldn't see what was behind them.

Perfect.

She found an opening in the material and tugged Emmett with her.

"What the hell are you doing?" His voice dominated the small space, where open cardboard boxes with a few remaining champagne glasses were stacked. Evidently they were using this area as storage.

"We should be safe hidden here unless they run out of glassware."

The fabric cast a blue light onto the planes of his angled face. So damn handsome.

"Stefanie."

"You can call me *queen*." She tugged his bow tie

free, and seeing that strip of untied silk lying on either side of his collar had lust pooling low in her belly. "Guess what you become when you marry the queen?"

She began unbuttoning his shirt. Three buttons down, he gripped her hand. But he did not stop her. Instead, he brushed his thumb along her skin and then loosened his hold.

Yes. He wanted this as much as she did.

She parted his shirt and exposed his glorious chest, pressing a kiss to his rock-solid pecs.

When she dragged her tongue to his abs, he caught her elbows like he was torn about allowing her to sink to her knees before him.

Tenderly, she laid her lips on his stomach and then teased the tip of her tongue past the waistline of his pants. She brushed his hold aside and worked his belt from its buckle. Emmett's hands hovered uselessly at his sides while his eyes burned twin holes into her.

Stefanie opened his zipper, pleased to find a hard ridge pushing against the seam of his boxer briefs. At least one part of his anatomy had no argument about what she was trying to do.

My accomplice.

She took him in her hand and Emmett's head dropped back on his neck. A moan of pleasure vibrated down his form, low enough that she barely heard it over the bumping bass outside their shrouded hiding place.

"Marrying the queen," she said as she tugged his pants and boxers past his heavy thighs, "makes you—" she flicked her tongue over the head of his erection "—the *king.*"

Opening her mouth wide to accommodate him, she took him onto her tongue and laved his soft flesh. He tasted *heavenly*, his masculine fragrance filling her nostrils as he filled her mouth.

His expelled breath was a gruff echo of her own pleasure as she hummed and took him deeper. She uncurled one of his fists and laid his flat palm on the back of her head, letting him know it was okay to encourage her.

He stood stiffly for a few seconds before giving in to the pleasure she was delivering. Then he let her do what she'd wanted to do since their wedding night.

Her husband was going to come *first* tonight.

She sucked the tip of his shaft, refusing to let up even when his knees locked and he growled her name.

"Stef." His voice was a rumble of far-off thunder. *"Stefanie."* That one, too, but closer. *Louder.*

She released him and locked her eyes on his, making the same request he had in the jewelry store when he bought their rings. "Let me."

He sent one concerned look at the curtain behind which they'd hidden, but before the conflict in his brain could ruin their fun, she took him on her tongue again.

Then he was no longer conflicted.

His hands encouraged her, his words praising her with gentle gruffness. "Yes, honey. Like that. Just like that."

He wound his fingers into her hair and tightened his grip pleasantly. She picked up the pace, spurred on by the popping threads of his control.

A moment later, he spilled his release into her mouth. She let him, relishing a moment that was about more than her winning, more than him coming first. She wanted him to know that he was as worthy of her as she was of him.

That they'd found forever in the unlikeliest of circumstances.

In that moment, on her knees behind the Sparkle & Shine gala, Stefanie allowed her heart to have a say.

It was just a whisper, but she recognized the four-letter word. A word that normally preceded marriage rather than following the vows.

She shut it out and rose to her feet, focusing on the here and now and the dazed look in her husband's eyes. But the blissful afterglow was short-lived when a familiar voice spoke from directly outside the curtain.

"Have you seen Stef and Emmett yet?" the voice asked.

"Not yet," a woman answered.

Emmett wrestled with his pants as Stefanie bit her lip to hide a laugh. He palmed her mouth to stifle that giggle, his brow a thundercloud of displeasure.

Evidently, Mayor Chase Ferguson was looking for them.

Twenty

Mimi assessed Emmett from one seahorse table away, her long lashes dipping to conceal the color of her eyes. Stefanie had been talking with her over champagne while Emmett and Chase found glasses of liquid that were *not* bubbly or French.

"What do you think they're talking about?" Chase asked.

Hopefully not Stef going down on me at this very party.

"No idea," Emmett answered. Chase appreciated honesty but he wouldn't appreciate *that* much honesty.

"How does Mimi make a simple red dress look so damn tempting? Is it midnight yet?" Chase's irritated tone made Emmett smile.

A decade back, Emmett had witnessed Chase fall over himself for Miriam Andrix. Neither Emmett nor Chase had been looking for anything permanent that summer. Emmett had indulged in a few very *im*permanent hookups, but not his best friend. No, Chase had followed Mimi around like a puppy. Then he'd let her go when she hadn't successfully fitted into the Ferguson family fold.

Emmett bristled as he considered how much he had in common with Chase's fiancée.

"...toast at midnight and then I'm getting the hell out of here," Chase was saying. He shot an elbow into Emmett's ribs. "Hey. What's up with you?"

"Never thought I'd see the day where you and Miriam were reunited," he said to conceal the deeper truth.

Chase's irritation faded in a blink. He was a man in love and it encompassed him and anyone around him whenever his future bride was near.

"You never thought I'd pull my head out of my ass, you mean?" Chase chuffed at his own expense before taking a drink of his whiskey. "I'm better with her in my life. Great, actually."

Miriam's attention was on Stefanie, who lifted her hand and gestured as she told a story. Her wedding ring caught the light and winked like a lighthouse warning Emmett away from the rocks.

Warnings he'd ignored since he placed that ring on her finger.

It's working. That's what I'm saying.

Stef tossed her head and laughed, and a ribbon of longing tied itself into a knot in his gut. She'd called him a king before lowering herself to her knees in front of him this evening. Every part of him had wanted to lift her into his arms and haul her very fine ass out of here. To finish what they'd started. To take her over the edge the way she had him.

His best friend's muttered curse brought him back to the present. Chase's expression was a mask of acceptance.

"I thought your attention to Stefanie over the years was about loyalty to our family. Or to me," he added with a grunt.

"It was," Emmett said before correcting with, "Is."

"What's in it for her?"

He knew what Chase was asking. What did Stefanie have to gain from this marriage? The way Chase saw it, the decks were unevenly stacked—in Emmett's favor.

"She can decide that for herself. You know where my loyalty lies."

"I know where it used to lie." Chase raised a sardonic eyebrow. "I've been usurped."

"She is the queen," Emmett murmured against the rim of his glass, unable to conceal a knowing smile. Chase didn't hear him. The countdown had started at the fifteen-second mark and the crowd had joined in.

Miriam rushed over to take Chase's hand and dragged him into the sea of partygoers. That left Stefanie and Emmett standing at separate tables eyeing each other through the melee.

She lifted her flute of champagne in silent cheers as the countdown raged on.

Five...

Four...

Emmett set aside his rocks glass and walked toward her, breaching the gap by half. She could meet him halfway if she wanted to. He wouldn't force her.

Three...

She started toward him, confidence making her eyes sparkle like her shimmery dress.

Two...

One!

With shouts of "Happy New Year" on the air, he scooped his wife into his arms and kissed her long and hard. The same way he would make love to her in his bed tonight.

In *their* bed tonight.

When they parted, her eyes glazed with lust as the gala's guests warbled along to "Auld Lang Syne."

His wife opened her mouth to join in, and her eyes never left his.

What he saw in their depths shook him to the core. Her aquamarine gaze revealed nothing short of adoration. Lust darkened her pupils, too, but beneath that there was more.

Much more than he'd anticipated.

She climbed to her toes, her warm breath brushing over his cheek. His balls tightened. He wanted this woman again already. When she whispered in his ear, he prayed that it'd be a request he could accommodate and not the three-word phrase she'd expect him to return.

But instead of that three-word bomb, she dropped a different one—one that sizzled his nerve endings and had him bolting for the door a nanosecond later. Three words shaped by the promise of her capable mouth.

"Take me home."

"I'm falling in love with him and I have no idea what to do." Stef barged into Penelope's office, the words exiting her mouth before she could register what she was seeing.

"Oh my God!" She slapped her hand over her eyes.

"Get the hell out!" Zach shouted before taking the Lord's name in vain in a more colorful way than she had. Unfortunately, the hand that covered her eyes had been the slightest bit delayed, so she'd gotten an eyeful of her brother's naked rear.

"I had an appointment!" Stef yelled, hand still protecting her retinas as she backed from the office. She shut the door as Penelope laughed, apparently finding this very unfunny situation hilarious.

"I'm sorry, Stef!" Pen called out around another laugh. "I lost track of the time."

Zach was still swearing. He also muttered something about how they needed to move farther away from his family, but Stefanie didn't think he meant that part.

Pen soothed him with words Stef couldn't make out, and when those words gave way to the telltale slurping sound of long kisses, Stef decided to help herself to something from the kitchen.

Conveniently, the kitchen was on the opposite side of the house, far away from her canoodling brother and sister-in-law.

More minutes than she would've liked to acknowledge later, her brother entered his kitchen, his nostrils flared and his hair a wreck. There was no sign of his always present "good ole boy" smile and dimple.

"I had an appointment," Stef insisted before munching another potato chip.

"She did." Penelope walked in behind Zach and pinched his butt. He spun around and kissed her, his smile and dimple returning.

Stef let out a wistful sigh.

"All right, all right. Let's give Stef a break." Pen patted his face and smiled.

"I have to go back to the office. See you tonight." His murmur was low and, yes, seductive. Stef hadn't missed that.

"As for you…" He turned to Stef, serious again. "I'm going to pretend I didn't hear what you said when you barged in there. I can't handle that right now."

"You! I'm the one who got a look at your full moon while you were in a very tender position with your wife. All you had to hear was my feelings for Emmett."

"No." Zach put his hands out in front of him as if that could keep her from saying any more offending words. "I have to go."

Once he was gone, she shook her head at Pen. "And you love him."

"As much as hot cocoa at Christmastime."

Stef had to agree that her favorite beverage during her favorite holiday was fabulous. "That's the best."

She munched another chip, but her sudden craving for cocoa ruined the salty bite.

Pen filled a water glass from a pitcher in the fridge and sat down at the breakfast bar beside her. "You're falling for your husband."

"I think so. Why are you shaking your head?"

Had Stefanie lost her one and only confidant? Did Pen think Stef was too young, too caught up, too *whatever* to know what love was?

"I've seen this happen before. This isn't my first time helping clients navigate a marriage of convenience, you know."

Hope flared in Stefanie's chest. "You mean…couples who started out like Emmett and me ended up staying together?"

She nodded. "I'm not saying I have the success rate of eHarmony or anything, but I have been invited to a *lot* of anniversary parties."

"Your shirt's buttoned wrong." Stef grinned.

"Brat." Pen winked to let Stef know she was kidding before rebuttoning her shirt. "Talk to me."

Stefanie did talk to her, and it came out in one long stream of consciousness diatribe.

"I'm falling in love with Emmett and I don't want to tell him because I'm afraid he'll freak out since we've been married for about thirty seconds. But how long is long enough to admit you're in love with someone? Am I supposed to draw up an agreement or contract about that, too? Is no one allowed to share their *feels* until we're sure Chase is reelected?"

"Oh my heavens. All right." Pen gripped Stefanie's shoulders. "Listen. You were sitting in this kitchen when Zach was considering buying me an island when he and I were on the rocks."

"True. He was racking his brain about how to win you back." Stef remembered it well. Her blockhead brother had no idea he was in love with Pen when it was obvious to anyone watching that he'd fallen for her so hard he was sick over it.

"That's partially my fault," Pen said.

"I could never blame you. Not when it's so much easier to blame my idiot brother." Stef smiled affectionately.

"I didn't tell Zach how I felt. He didn't know I loved him. We could've saved some heartbreak if I'd been honest."

"But it worked out in the end." At the time Pen had been pregnant with Olivia and was juggling her entire life around a pretend engagement to Zach. Who could blame her for clamming up?

"How does Emmett feel?"

"Well, he loves going to bed with me."

"God in heaven" came a gruff, pained voice. "Forgot my keys," Zach called from the foyer. "I'm leaving now."

The door opened and shut and Stefanie shook her head. "He's so screwed when Olivia is old enough to date."

"Luckily, we have many, *many* years before that possibility." Pen smiled. "You and Emmett are compatible physically...but is there more?"

"For me there is, but it's probably best to wait to tell him how I feel. Just a little while. Until I'm sure that it's real."

Pen nodded. "In your circumstances, I think that's very smart. You don't want to go off half-cocked and then realize you were wrapped up in the moment."

"Right. Okay." Stef felt better already. "So...how long should I wait?"

"Not too long. Follow your heart."

"My gut's more reliable."

"Then follow your gut. You've got this."

Twenty-One

"I miss Oscar." Stefanie looked cute slumped in a padded chair at the classy downtown restaurant.

Sunday had stopped to pick up her beloved cat this morning, which also happened to be Sunday. The second his ex left his town house, Stefanie had thrown her arms around him and announced they were going to brunch.

He couldn't argue. Not after his wife had dealt with his ex-girlfriend and was forced to say goodbye to her temporary cat.

The first sip of coffee hit his tongue like battery acid. "What the hell?"

"It's vanilla cinnamon. Their house specialty," Stef chirped.

"It's repulsive."

She tsk-tsked and reached over to touch the corner of his frown. He waved the waitress over while Stef accused him of being a "spoilsport" and requested coffee that *didn't* taste like a Christmas tree was sitting in his mug.

"Salmon Benedict. How yummy does that sound?" Stef asked as she perused the one-sheet menu.

He was ordering *off* the menu. He didn't want foie gras with baby greens or savory pancakes with chives. He wanted coffee—unflavored, thank you very much—two eggs over easy and three slices of whole-wheat toast.

He still didn't understand the concept of "brunch." A first meal was *breakfast*. Period. No matter what time it was eaten.

About twenty minutes later, Emmett was in the midst of changing his mind.

He dug into his eggs over easy and found himself enjoying "brunch" with his wife.

Her stack of waffles resembled the Leaning Tower of Pisa, and he begrudgingly admired her technique of syrup and butter application. He polished off his plate, finished hers when she said she was full and leaned back to palm his very satisfied stomach as the waitress refilled his coffee mug.

"How's Chase's campaign going?" Stef asked, hands wrapped around her Christmas potion.

"You didn't ruin his chances, if that's what you're asking," Emmett said after a furtive look around.

They weren't news any longer. Two weeks of wedded bliss later and everyone was bored of them. According to Penelope, the Dallas Duchess was too busy reporting on dating Blake Eastwood *herself*, if that could be believed.

Who knew what was real anymore?

Except Emmett was beginning to suspect his own marriage was realer than anyone knew. As such, there was something he needed to tell Stefanie that he hadn't come clean about yet.

"I told him, by the way," he said.

"Told…Chase? Told him what?"

"No. I told my dad."

Her eyes widened. He went quiet while the waitress cleared their table and dropped off the check. Once she'd gone, Emmett rested his hands on his thighs and watched Stefanie carefully.

"You talked to your dad?"

"He called the mayor's office and left a message. He'd heard about the wedding and wanted to know if it was true. I don't tell him much. I never confide in him. But this… You're important."

He could see on her face what that meant to her—that he'd march into territories unknown for her. That he'd put himself in a position of discomfort for her. He would. *Repeatedly*, and for as long as she asked him to.

"I wanted Dad to hear the truth and I wanted him to hear it from me."

"That must've been hard for you." Her brow crimped. Concerned for him still. She was amazing.

"I know I haven't had many nice things to say about him but I don't think he's interested in your money. Even if he was, I'd never let him touch a red cent."

"Emmett." Stef's expression broadcast sincerity. "I don't think that. But if he needed it—"

"He doesn't." Emmett reclaimed his mug. "He said he hoped we were happy."

He took a drink, aware that the conversation was on hold. A glance at his wife's unreadable expression proved him right.

"Are you…?" He paused, not sure he wanted an answer. "Happy?"

She leaned forward and put her hand on his arm. "Yes."

So trusting. So beautiful. And all his.

For now.

"You okay?" he asked when Stefanie's eyes filled with concern.

"No. I mean, yes." She pulled her hand away and folded her hands in her lap. She blew out a breath, her eyes on the crumbs on the table in front of her.

"Stef?"

She met his eyes and blurted out, "I'm in love with you."

His world stopped on a dime, the restaurant fading into the background, the world canting to one side like an earthquake had opened the ground beneath them.

"My feelings for you tipped into L-word territory a while ago. I was waiting to tell you until the right moment. I guess that's now," she mumbled at the edge of her mug. "It's not like it's going away."

"Stefanie."

"I know." She closed her eyes. *"I know."*

At the idea of this being more—of having more—every part of him bristled. He couldn't love her the way she needed to be loved—the way she *deserved* to be loved. His past was dark, the cracks filled in with loss and distance. He couldn't ask her to be a permanent part of his life.

Stefanie *was* life. Life and verve and wealth. She was Ferguson royalty. Emmett...wasn't.

Even as he resisted, his mind played a motion picture of what it could mean to love his wife—a wife who loved him.

Them living in his town house or a house that they bought together. A daughter with blond ringlets, a son who would never know the meaning of neglect. Making love to Stefanie in the morning. Making love to Stefanie in the evening. Showering her with affection and gifts and serving at her pleasure…

But then he considered the rest of her family. Chase had warned Emmett not to let her get too close. How far would he take it when he learned how Stef felt? Would the mayor fire his head of security? And if Emmett lost his job, then what would he do? He wouldn't let Stefanie support both of them.

The idea of being a husband who didn't live up to his responsibilities, who was unable to provide for his wife—was abhorrent.

Even if he acknowledged his dormant feelings—even if he uncovered that he felt a dangerous combination of love and respect for her alongside the terror of losing her—he would ignore those feelings.

He'd ignore what he felt for her because she deserved better than the pittance he could offer.

He'd made a habit of living in the present. He didn't look back. He didn't look forward. And *presently*, they had a marriage based on convenience and a hell of a lot of attraction.

That was it.

His big heart suffered another fissure knowing he'd have to let her go. Knowing that for him, goodbye would leave another permanent scar of loss in his soul. But he had plenty of memories. He'd forever be grateful for the time he'd spent with her.

That, as much as it ached him to the bone, would have to be enough.

Her husband had turned to stone at her announcement. Emmett glared at his cooling coffee as if attempting to heat it with laser vision.

She'd considered keeping the fact that she loved him to herself, but she was tired of keeping things to herself. She was *tired* of playing it safe where he was concerned. She'd let her brother's election hold her back—let it keep her from doing what she really wanted for long enough.

Emmett had stepped *way* out of his comfort zone to contact his dad about her. And then he'd told her that she was important, and by the time he'd made vows to protect the Ferguson fortune and her well-being... Well, she'd been swept up.

Clarity blew in like a fierce storm. She finally knew what she wanted. And what she wanted was to stay married.

Emmett didn't mention her "I love you" on the drive home from the restaurant. She hadn't expected him to, but she'd be lying if she said she wouldn't have leaped for joy if he had offered up an "I love you, too."

In his kitchen, she dropped her purse on the counter and watched as Emmett hung his keys on the hook by the door. He barely glanced her way when he walked by.

"Hey." She touched his arm.

He turned, his eyes slowly climbing from her hand to her face.

"You probably have to sit with this for a while. *I've* been sitting with it for a while," she said. "I know it seems fast, but we've done something remarkable. We were married. We're living as husband and wife after knowing each other for a decade. This is something worth exploring and I don't want you to talk yourself out of it." She ran her fingers down his arm and squeezed his hand. "You can take your time deciding how you feel about me. I won't force it, and I won't pout because you didn't say it back."

"That's enough." His voice was gruff. "That's enough talk about how you feel and how I feel and how this is going to work out. This is temporary. This has always been temporary."

"Things change."

"You couldn't possibly know that you love me after only—"

"Do *not* finish that sentence. I'm sick to death of people questioning my heart and my will—both of which are *mine*. Both of which I am the authority on. I, of all people, know how I feel about *you*."

On a deep sigh, he came to her, but not out of anger and not to argue with her. Instead he pulled her close and dropped his forehead on hers. His eyes sank closed and she wrapped her arms around his waist, holding on to him as well as to the hope that this meant he accepted how she felt about him.

He didn't have to say it back—she'd meant that—but she wouldn't stand for him, for anyone, contesting how she felt. Not ever again.

"I need a nap." He put a kiss on her forehead.

"Okay."

He walked into the living room and she stood in the center of the kitchen wondering what the hell to do with herself now.

"I'm going out…to do a little shopping."

"Okay," he called as he stretched out on the sofa.

Retail therapy had always cleared her head in the past, and right now her head couldn't be foggier.

Twenty-Two

In the week since I-Love-You-gate, Stefanie had gone shopping...a lot.

Since she'd been raiding every boutique within a thirty-mile radius, she decided to put a few of her new things—furniture, dress, champagne glasses—to good use and have a girls' night in.

She'd been practically buried in Emmett's world and had started missing her own. Namely, her apartment decor, which she might have taken to the extreme. She'd spotted a shimmery throw pillow and decided to redecorate everything in gold and white. Clean, comfy lines and crisp, bright, clean colors.

Hence the new white leather sofa, gold-and-white leopard-print ottoman, gilt-framed mirror, gold candles and sheer white curtains.

Yes, she'd done *plenty* of shopping.

Champagne poured, Stefanie glided into the living

room with a tray of stemmed glasses. Pen sat on the ottoman, her white pantsuit pristine and fitting in nicely with Stef's new living room, and Mimi was dressed as per her usual in bright jewel tones. She sat on the sofa in a no-muss-no-fuss pair of slim dark denim jeans and ruby-red sweater.

"You do know how to entertain," she praised, taking a flute from the tray and pushing a lock of her wavy dark hair behind her ear.

"Is this new?" Pen patted the ottoman with one hand before taking her own flute.

"Yes. The couch, too." Stef set the tray on the coffee table, a clear acrylic one she'd bought last year. See? She'd kept a few things!

"Hmm." Pen tapped the glass with her fingernail and looked around.

"*Hmm*, what?" But Stef was pretty sure she knew.

"It's interesting that you're buying new furniture for your place. I was under the impression you were staying with Emmett."

"I am." Stef smoothed her hand over the middle cushion and sat, aware of Mimi's raised brow of interest. "I had to have this sofa, and white isn't exactly in Emmett's color scheme at his place."

"I like it," Mimi said. Kindly. "Thank you for inviting me out. I don't spend enough time with you two."

"Sorry about that," Pen said with a wince. "I'm so busy with work and Olivia. I haven't been prioritizing my friends—or my family."

"Totally understandable." Mimi, ever the laid-back one, brushed the topic aside with a hand. "It's nice to do something girlie that doesn't require hiking boots."

Miriam worked in Dallas at the Conservation Society. She had a history of protesting the oil industry, which had caused some bumps in the road between her and Chase—*and a certain pain-in-the-keister Dallas blogger*, Stef thought with an eye roll. But Miriam wasn't only tough and opinionated, she was also lovely and had added the perfect bevel to Chase's straight-edge.

"That said…" Mimi eased back onto the sofa, crossing an arm over her waist and propping the hand holding her champagne flute. "What's *really* going on with your marriage to Emmett, Stef?"

"I not only suspect you have formed your own opinions," Stefanie answered, "I also assume that my marriage is a frequent topic of discussion in the Chase Ferguson mansion."

Mimi had relocated from Montana and moved in with Chase almost instantaneously. Stef had always been amazed by that—the way her future sister-in-law had turned away from her life in Montana for him. Although Chase owned a drop-dead gorgeous Montana lake house, so it wasn't as if they'd never go back. They'd decided to have their wedding in the mansion, but the date was on hold due to—what else?—Chase's campaign.

"Chase might've brought up your names a few times." Mimi gave her a coy smile. "I understand what it's like to leave everything behind and move into a man's house." She nodded as she took in the living room. "I *also* understand the desire to have your own space."

"As do I." Pen's tone could only be described as droll. "When Zach bought me out of my lease, I felt evicted from my own life. Good thing I love that man." But her smile warmed at the memory. At the time Pen hadn't felt *warmly* about Zach's heavy hand, but it'd been his way of showing he loved her.

"You two are meant to be, and Olivia is a princess," Miriam said approvingly. "I love Chase. I have always loved Chase." Her gaze softened on a distant point in the room before snapping back to Stef. "When you're in love it makes the compromise worth it."

"Only when you are *both* in love. With each other," Stef murmured into her delicate flute. She swallowed the rest of her champagne before grabbing the bottle and pouring herself a refill. When she offered her guests the same, she found both women eyeing her with interest.

"You're in love with him," Mimi said matter-of-factly.

"She has been for a while," Pen confirmed. "She busted into my office, and caught Zach on top of me with his pants down, to announce how much she loved Emmett."

"Scarred for life," Stef said, and everyone giggled, including her.

"Have you told him?" Miriam asked.

With a deep sigh of acceptance, Stef confirmed that she had. "He didn't react. We finished our brunch and drove home and then he took a nap."

"A nap!" Mimi's outrage satisfied a part of Stefanie that felt the same way.

"*Yes.* And then he told me that I couldn't be sure how I felt this soon."

"Oh *hell* no." Pen helped herself to more champagne. "He has no right to tell you what you feel. No one does. Only you can know that."

"Exactly what I keep telling Chase." Mimi held up her glass and Pen emptied the last of the champagne into it. "Your oldest brother is so protective of you, Stef. Too protective. But…I understand why."

"Traitor!" Stef playfully accused.

"Ugh. I know. I hate that I understand him, but, hon, I do." At least Miriam had the decency to sound apologetic. "Emmett and Chase have been friends for a long time. Emmett has been at your brother's side—at your *family's* side—for years. For him to take advantage of you after—"

"*I* was the one who proposed!" Stef didn't mean to shout, but she was fed up with everyone thinking she was a helpless little girl in need of coddling. "*I* was the one who asked him to marry me. *I* was the one who dragged him to city hall. Emmett slept on the floor of that B and B until our wedding night. Even then he approached me carefully. He's been nothing but careful," she said, her voice softening. "He's been gentle and giving and protective. I thought he was feeling more for me than the physical, but if he is, he's keeping it to himself."

"He probably doesn't know," Pen said, then added an eye roll and an explanation. "Zach."

"Great point." Zach had had no idea he was head over heels for Penelope until Stef had sat in front of him and forced him to admit it.

"Chase left me. *Left!* He flew back to Texas and left me crying in my apartment," Mimi said, joining in to air her own grievances. "On the plane ride home Emmett helped him understand that Chase was as in love with me as I was with him."

"Emmett did that?" Stef had never heard this story. She tried to picture Emmett convincing practical Chase to fight for something as impractical as true love and failed.

"It's easier to see it in others than in yourself. He probably has no idea how he feels."

Then someone should make him see it.

Maybe *Stef* should make him see it.

There was more to them than sex and a shared bedroom. Emmett was in denial for reasons she hadn't figured out yet, but it was high time he fessed up to what he was thinking.

If he hadn't realized how he felt yet, then she'd provide an opportunity for him to do just that.

"My mother has an art show at her house on Saturday," Stef said, a light bulb clicking on over her head.

"Don't remind me." Miriam wrinkled her nose. "I'm sorry. I didn't mean for that to sound disrespectful. Your mother and I have only recently mastered 'cordial' when we're side by side. An evening spent with her and the Dallas elite brings forth a serious case of the don't-wannas for me."

"Believe me, I get it." Stef had to laugh. "Just be yourself, Mimi. That's the secret with a crowd like that. When you don't put on airs they know you don't care and respect you more."

"She's right," Penelope, who'd had her own experience in the limelight, said. "It wasn't so long ago I was at your fiancé's birthday party and every pair of eyes were on me when Zach announced to everyone that we were *engaged*. Know what I did? I ate pear-gorgonzola salad and lamb and then I danced with Zach. We caused quite the scandal, but I was content to let the crowd think whatever they wanted."

While Mimi and Pen chatted, Stef was busy thinking whatever *she* wanted. Like how she planned on proving to Emmett that what he felt for her was love and nothing short of it.

* * *

Elle Ferguson's art show was in full swing. The massive house was filled with women dripping with jewelry, and men drinking enough scotch to dull the pain when it came time to surrender their wallets.

Emmett wasn't bankrolling tonight, but he was drinking scotch.

Zach ambled over, his own lowball glass filled with brown liquid, his assessing gaze taking in Emmett's position in the corner.

"Is it your security background that has you holding up a wall and keeping an eye on the crowd, or is it that you don't want to mingle with any of these stiffs?"

"Bit of both."

Zach positioned himself next to Emmett and scanned the crowd. Zach's wife was among them, admiring a painting with Stefanie by her side. Emmett had always thought Penelope was a beautiful woman, but even in a white floor-length gown with her pale blond hair in a twist, Penelope couldn't hold a candle to the beauty Emmett's wife possessed.

Stefanie's blue dress reminded him of the color of her eyes. Shimmering with secrets he wanted to uncover. Since the afternoon brunch where she'd mentioned she was in love with him, Emmett had been playing it cool. He acted on the outside like he hadn't thought another thing about it when, in reality, it was *all* he'd been able to think about.

Earning the heart of a woman you'd never imagined being this close to was humbling. And terrifying when what he had to give back was so little.

"Think she'll buy it?" Emmett nodded toward the painting where their wives stood.

God, that was still weird to think about. Emmett had a *wife*. Even an impermanent one.

An impermanent one who loves you.

"Given that a majority of the proceeds go to charity, I'm positive Penelope is going to buy something. Hell if I know what she's going to do with it. The last time we came to one of these I had no idea what she'd purchased until it was delivered and hung in our living room." Zach shrugged, embodying affable charm and laid-back ease. He definitely had that side to him, and since he'd slid a ring onto Penelope's finger and vowed to be hers forever, that side of him had expanded.

The right woman could make a man better.

Before Emmett could chew on that thought for too long, Zach spoke again.

"Anything new with you and my sister?"

"Why do I have the feeling you know something?" Emmett shot Zach a raised eyebrow.

Miriam, Penelope and Stef had spent an evening together not too long ago. No doubt Emmett's name had come up.

"If you think Pen would come home and tell me what they talked about, you don't know her. Pen and Stef were thick before Pen and I were." His smirk turned cunning. "Well. *Almost* before Pen and I were."

"There's nothing new to report." Emmett sipped his scotch and forgave himself for the lie.

To his surprise, Zach didn't try to pry information out of him or threaten him like Chase had. They talked about football, about how much money their wives would spend tonight and then about getting together for dinner soon. It was the most reasonable, and possibly the longest, conversation Emmett had ever had with Zach. He could get used to having another Ferguson in his corner.

Penelope moved on to another painting and waved Zach over for his opinion. Stef caught Emmett's eye and smiled before becoming tied up in a conversation with an older woman in front of a sculpture in the corner.

A *hideous* sculpture. One Emmett hoped to hell didn't end up in his house.

Moving across the room to refill his scotch, he imagined Stefanie buying it and what she might say when she brought it home.

"You are not storing that thing here," he'd tell her.

"It's not a thing. It's a work of art."

"It's horrifying and it'll give me nightmares."

"You'll love it because you love me."

The imaginary conversation made him smile at first but as he pictured the end of it, him agreeing that he did love her and telling her as much, the cord stringing his heart to the center of his chest snapped.

Like a shot, he realized he was in too deep.

After brunch he hadn't been any closer to throwing out an "I love you, too" in spite of Stef's profession. He'd thought that had spoken volumes. Hell, he didn't know if he was *capable* of love—not of the long-lasting variety.

But he loved her. Of that he was sure. It rang in his gut, tuning fork true, and caused a falling sensation that sent his stomach into his throat.

Chase had warned him about Stefanie having feelings for him. That if it was unequal in any way, Emmett was to walk away.

But what if it was equal? What if he was in love with her and wanted a life with her? What would Chase say then? And how would Stefanie's parents react? Already they'd expressed their displeasure that she'd married Emmett Keaton. No doubt they'd prefer someone with blue blood to enter into the Ferguson family rather than someone with a blue collar.

He was embarrassed to admit that until just now, he'd been thinking of what he could lose—of all he could lose—but he hadn't considered what Stef might lose.

If she dug in her heels and decided to be stubborn, if she was as in love with him as she'd claimed—she'd never walk away no matter how her parents or her brothers felt about the permanent union.

"Sir, may I get you a refill?" a passing waiter asked.

Emmett blinked out of his epiphany and handed over his empty glass. "Scotch. Neat. You know what? Make it a double."

Because the conclusion that Emmett had just drawn was not a pretty one.

Stefanie might choose him.

Over her family.

Losing the Fergusons pained him more than he could fathom, but he refused to let Stefanie lose them, too.

How far would Chase take his threats? If Emmett defied him—defied Stef's entire family—would they cut her out? Would she be left on the outside, like his mother was by her family when she'd married Van?

He couldn't imagine any of them drawing that line, but *Stefanie* might.

For him.

Because she loved him.

No. He would never allow her to know a life of loss and heartache. He'd never maroon Stefanie on an island with himself as her only refuge.

Even though he loved her. *Especially* because he loved her.

That thought filled him with both hope and devastation. Evidently he was far more capable of loving than he'd ever imagined... And yet he couldn't allow himself to stay. Not when Stefanie could lose everything.

The waiter brought over a double scotch, and with a shaking hand, Emmett downed most of it in one burning swallow. He'd never ask Stefanie to live without her family. To sacrifice her stakes in Ferguson Oil; to give up the life she knew to slum it with a guy from the wrong side of town. No matter how much wealth he'd gained or how hard he'd worked to get to where he was, it didn't change where he was from.

With that realization came a healthy dose of sad acceptance. As much as he loved her, he wouldn't ask her to choose—or risk her losing her family for him. This room of richies was a timely reminder of how he didn't fit in here or at brunch or beside any of them. And Stef didn't belong with him, either.

She'd see the truth of it after a month or a year. She'd grow tired of his quiet nature and flat sense of style. She'd want someone as vibrant and lively as her and he would never measure up.

She'd miss her family.

She'd told him that marrying a queen made him king, but what if it was the opposite? What if him marrying a queen made her a commoner?

Stefanie was too vibrant to ever be common.

He wouldn't let her stay and try to change his mind.

But he would minimize her suffering.

He would end this farce with her family around so she'd have shoulders to cry on—people who loved her and could take care of her while the man who loved her the most did what was best for her.

He'd walk away.

She deserved no less and he'd be selfish to expect more.

A flash of blue sparkled toward him and Emmett's stomach made a quick trip to his toes. There was no better time than the present—and her entire family was already here.

Twenty-Three

Her husband looked foxy in black pants, a pressed white shirt and the patterned black-and-turquoise tie she'd bought to match her dress. He looked *so* good, in fact, Stefanie was considering dragging him into one of the bedrooms of her mother's massive home.

But her steps faltered as she grew closer and noticed that Emmett's face was a mask of hard lines.

"Yikes. What happened to you? Did Mrs. Morrison ask you for a donation for the city statue? She's been hitting up everyone this evening. Dad had to tell her to stop twice."

Emmett watched her darkly, his jaw sawing back and forth before he opened his mouth and said something she never thought she'd hear. "I love that you love me."

His words were gravel laden and accompanied by a pained expression that didn't match what she felt upon hearing them. She was…*elated*. Cloud nine wasn't high enough. All the complicated feelings that arose whenever she was in bed with him or next to him in the car or at his side converged into one indelible fact: she was married and in love with her husband…and he was on the cusp of admitting he was in love with her, too.

Her smile emerged, filling her with warmth, but his next words were ice-cold.

"I want an annulment."

"An…annulment?"

"Or a dissolution." He gulped the scant bit of remaining liquid in his glass. "Whichever one means I want nothing from you."

"What are you talking about?" She was tempted to pinch herself to find out if she'd slipped into a dream. No, a *nightmare*. But this was real. As real as the guests at the party, who were carrying on their conversations and refilling their drinks as if Stefanie's world wasn't crumbling around her.

Emmett had just told her he wanted *nothing* from her. How could that be when she wanted *everything* from him?

"I don't understand," she tried again. "You don't want to stay married to me?"

She was missing something. Unless…

"Did Zach threaten you? Did he—"

"This is my decision, Stefanie." Emmett's tone was dry, his face set in stone. "I can't let you continue in a marriage where you feel more for me than I'm capable of returning."

"I'm the one who decides that." Her voice was thick with grief. Shaking with fear. The pain came next as realization set in.

He was done with her. Done with *them*.

"I agreed to marry you for one reason. It's my job to protect you."

"Your *job* is to protect my brother, the mayor. Your right, your *privilege*, is to love the woman who loves you."

Tears welled in her eyes as the pain pummeled her with rapid-fire punches to the heart. Emmett's expression told her all she needed to know. He didn't love her. Not in the way she wanted—the way she needed. He felt loyalty to her because she was a Ferguson, because he was duty bound, but he was no closer to giving her his heart than before they were married.

His next words eviscerated her.

"It was a privilege to be yours."

The ugly flare of hope fizzled out instantaneously. *Was.*

He was saying he wasn't hers any longer.

"You still don't believe you're worthy of me." Tears trembled on the edge of her lashes. "I already told you—"

"You don't know all there is to know about me." His angry tone cut into her. "I grew up as poor as the families in attendance at your charity Christmas dinners. My family wasn't from a wealthy section of Dallas. Hell, we weren't middle-class. I didn't grow up in a fancy neighborhood with college savings. I lived in a house with a dilapidated roof, a termite problem and a yard the size of a stamp."

"Do you think I care where you came from?"

"No. I don't. And that's the problem. I'm a man who can't possibly be what you need me to be. You're an heiress to the goddamn Ferguson fortune and I *serve* at the pleasure of the mayor of Dallas."

His raised voice carried on the air—no doubt the entire guest list had heard every word.

"I love you for who you are, Emmett. Not for who you were."

He stepped forward and for one fleeting second she saw a dab of hope in his eyes. She sensed that he wanted to let go, lean in and commit to her forever and ever, amen.

But that hope was dashed a second later.

And his words were the final straw.

"I'll never not be the guy who lost half his family on Christmas day. I'll never not be from a broken family and a poor home. I'll never fit in at art shows where you spend tens of thousands of dollars on shit like that—" he gestured to the painting nearest him as a few guests let out astounded gasps "—rather than buy something for someone who needs it." He sent a scathing look down her dress that made her feel self-conscious. "Your heart's in the right place, Stefanie. You are giving and loving and care about people. But I'm not one of your charity cases. And I won't stay in a marriage that never should have happened in the first place."

Witnessing Stefanie's rage was helping him through his speech. He wanted her angry. *Anger*, he could take. *Anger*, he knew what to do with. He'd been empowered by anger years ago. It'd driven him to become a strong man rather than curl up next to his father on the couch and gather dust. Anger was an action. And if Stef needed to be angry to accept what he was telling her, he'd gladly be her target.

He'd warmed up for the felling blow, so he might as well get to it.

"We're nothing alike. You eat at five-hundred-dollars-per-plate charity auctions and buy dresses you wear once and replace all the furniture in your house because you had a bad day."

Stef blanched. Out of the corner of his eye he saw Chase breaking through the crowd and coming at him full steam ahead.

Fine by Emmett; he was almost done.

"We're over. This. Is. Over."

She blinked and tears streamed down her face, but a diamond-hard glint shone in her eyes. His wife. So strong.

"You can't stand here and tell me you don't feel anything."

He was tempted to lie to her but he couldn't. Not even to spare her feelings. He valued her too much— and what she knew in her heart. After she'd worked this hard to be independent and gain confidence in herself, he wouldn't rob her of it.

"I didn't feel enough." His lip curled, his gut somersaulting as the anger faded from Stef's expression and hurt replaced it. "I'll send your things to your apartment."

He turned away before more tears spilled down Stefanie's cheeks, but he heard the gut-wrenching sob that climbed her throat. It was enough to weaken his knees and his resolve—but he couldn't afford to take it back.

He'd done this *for* her.

Grateful for Zach and Chase, Penelope and Miriam, Emmett left comforting Stefanie to her capable family. The Fergusons always tended to their own.

It was a mistake to believe he ever could be one of them.

Twenty-Four

Annulment.

No. *Dissolution.*

That was what Emmett had asked for. Whichever one would leave them both blameless.

Well, *tough.*

Stefanie couldn't stop blaming him. He was the one to blame! Another tear tumbled onto the cardboard box she was unpacking. Her things had arrived today via courier. She hadn't left much at Emmett's place. Only a few toiletries, sleepwear and—oh yeah—her stupid heart. She sifted through the box again, but there was no sign of the necessary organ.

She'd entertained a few scenarios—one involving keying his SUV, another taking a baseball bat to the headlights in true Carrie Underwood fashion, but Stef's rage had been eclipsed by pain.

When they'd entered into a marriage it'd been with

an understanding: that they would say "I do" and walk away when it was time. Now that he'd lured her in, made her love him and then took away her choice of staying, she regretted proposing. She couldn't see an ounce of good that could come of his leaving her decimated in a roomful of her family and her family's friends.

She stopped rummaging through the box, reminded by the shards of regret that her heart was right where it should be—eating a hole through her chest like battery acid. She hated herself for falling in love with him.

A dissolution made the most sense. She'd been completely disillusioned by their marriage.

After Emmett had left the party, her brothers and Penelope and Mimi surrounded Stef in a semicircle. Once they were sure she was okay, Chase had started for the door. She'd stopped him with a plea.

"Chase, please don't."

He'd turned to argue, but the anger in his expression quickly faded to concern for her.

"Please," she'd repeated.

She didn't need her brother taking up for her any longer. She didn't need to cause any more problems like, oh, say, Chase punching out Emmett in her mother's driveway. Besides, what good would it have done? It wouldn't have changed Emmett's mind. Just as she hadn't been able to change his mind about loving her. About making their marriage work.

And so Chase had stayed at the party and the Dallas Duchess didn't have the scoop on the dysfunctional billionaire Fergusons stepping in it yet again.

Stef was grateful for one thing—that Chase's reputation was in fine standing. His campaign was in full swing, the polls in his favor. It looked like he would still be mayor come May…which couldn't come soon enough.

She longed to skip forward a few months. To pass over the valley of the shadow of hurt and arrive at a place of peace and acceptance.

That kind of closure was an impossibility in three days' time. It was impossible for three *weeks'* time.

Hopefully it'd be a distant memory in three months. It'd better not take longer than three months. If it did she was going to move to the mountains and live in a yurt.

Emmett believed he didn't belong with her, that he couldn't love her the way she loved him. He'd been raised by a cold, disconnected father and evidently her soon-to-be ex-husband was a chip off the old ice block.

"Can I top you off?" Mimi carried in a thermos of homemade hot cocoa. It was too early in the afternoon for wine, and the warmth and sweetness of the cocoa had set Stefanie's innards at ease, if not her heart and mind. Warm innards would have to do.

Chase and Miriam had stopped by to check on her and Stef was so glad to see them, she'd promptly burst into tears. At least *they* loved her.

Chase carried in a tin of fancy homemade marsh-mallows. His eyebrows were bent in distress. Stef was the one problem he couldn't seem to fix.

"I'm so sorry, Chase." Her chin wobbled but she re-fused to cry anymore. Emmett was testing her limits, but she was tougher than this.

"Don't apologize for anything." His voice unyield-ing, as per his usual. The mayor of Dallas was nothing if not decisive.

"Worry about yourself, babe." That came from

Miriam. She popped a marshmallow into her mouth as she sat next to Stefanie on the couch.

"I'm going to his house. Do you have anything I need to drop off to him?"

"Sure. You can give him this." Stef held up her middle finger and Mimi chuckled.

Chase's smile was sad—sad for her.

"I don't have anything to say to the man who feels nothing for me."

"He didn't say that," Mimi said.

"Close enough." Stef slurped a melting marshmallow off the surface of her cocoa.

Chase muttered something that sounded like "That thickheaded prick" before grabbing his coat off the back of a chair.

"I don't want him to love me because my big brother threatened him," Stefanie told Chase.

"He resigned as head of security yesterday," he said. "I'm discussing that. Not you. I'm not interested in changing his mind if he feels nothing for you."

"You wouldn't want him anywhere near me if he was madly in love with me, either," she half joked.

"That's not true." Chase's eyes were narrowed, serious. "You deserve someone who knows your worth. It's all I've ever wanted for you. An arranged marriage—worse, one for the sake of my campaign—isn't what you deserve." A flicker of guilt colored his handsome features.

"Thank you."

"He's been smarter since he realized he's in love with me." Mimi winked at Stef and then looked up at her fiancé with adoration.

"You love him in equal measure, Mimi," Stef said. "We all see it."

Stefanie's heart ached for her own love lost at the same time it swelled to include the pure joy on her future sister-in-law's face. Enough of this wallowing. Mourning what could've been was a waste of time. There was too much good in the world to celebrate.

"Speaking of 'I do'—" Stef set aside her cocoa and faced Mimi on her sofa "—let's talk about your upcoming wedding. Have you found a dress? Who's your planner? What color bridesmaid dress will I wear?"

Mimi let out a sheepish laugh. "I do have wedding magazines in my purse…just in case."

"Good." Stef smiled through her hurt, determined to feel good instead of lousy for a few minutes. "Let's see them."

"I'll be back to pick you up after…after," Chase tacked on ominously before he kissed his future wife on the lips.

"No fighting," Stef warned him as he dropped a kiss on her forehead.

But his smirk and wink before he walked out the door told her that her warning had fallen on deaf ears.

Twenty-Five

Emmett trudged into the kitchen and opened the fridge, studying the paltry offerings. A box of pizza from two nights ago was wedged onto the shelf, balanced on a carton that used to hold six bottles of beer but now held two. Besides pizza and beer he had some cheese—moldy; lunch meat—scary; and eggs—not expired.

"Eggs for dinner, it is." Carton in hand, he walked to the stovetop, but when he bent to grab a skillet from a low cabinet, the world slipped off its axis. At least his world did.

That'd been happening a lot lately. It was like he was living on a damn Tilt-A-Whirl.

Since he'd called it quits with Stefanie three nights ago, he'd found a new weight to haul around in place of the fear of not being enough for her. A heavy, burdensome load that sat in the pit of his stomach like a cannonball.

Or a wrecking ball. That was how he felt.

Fucking *wrecked.*

All of a sudden his stomach soured at the idea of food. He shoved the carton of eggs back onto their shelf and reached for a beer at the same time his phone vibrated in his pocket.

Chase.

Emmett would finally face him. He'd expected his best friend to come sooner, and come in hot, his temper preceding him. Instead, Chase had accepted Emmett's leaving without fanfare.

It made sense. Chase had promised he'd choose Stefanie, which was what Emmett had wanted him to do. Emmett had emailed his resignation letter yesterday, which had solved another problem for his best friend. Chase wouldn't be forced to fire his head of security.

I'm in your driveway, the text read.

Come in, Emmett typed back. He opened the fridge and pulled out a second bottle of beer, setting it beside the other and popping off the caps.

Seconds later, Chase stepped into the kitchen and took one look at him, and his mouth flattened into a mirthless line.

"I opened you a beer." Emmett gestured, but before he had a chance to lift his own bottle and suck down half its contents, pain bloomed over his left cheekbone in a neon flash.

Blinking, he palmed his face and stared in astonishment at his houseguest. Chase's face was neutral, and if he hadn't been shaking out his hand, Emmett would've sworn he'd imagined the sucker punch.

"Should've expected your head to be that hard after what you pulled with Stef." Chase winced as he flexed his hand.

Emmett blinked, his vision finally clearing. "Expected this three days ago. You're late."

"My baby sister is in tears and it's your fault."

Emmett's chest caved in. "Still?"

He *hated* that she'd cried—that she was still crying. And because of him? Shouldn't she be over him by now, or at the very least shouldn't she accept that she'd dodged a bullet?

Chase came toward him, but Emmett was ready this time. Emmett ducked and Chase's fist swiped the air. Emmett landed a clumsy sock to Chase's gut, but it hit hard enough that Emmett steadied his best friend when it took the wind from his lungs.

Chase recovered quickly, ramming Emmett in the belly with his shoulder and smashing his back against the stainless steel fridge door.

"You son of a bitch." Chase pressed his forearm against Emmett's throat. "Do you have any idea what you cost her? What you took from her? And for what? So you could fuck her?"

Incensed, Emmett traded their positions, pressing Chase's back to the fridge. He raised his fist, poised to ruin the mayor's perfect nose, but then stopped cold, the taste of blood—or maybe that wrecking ball weight of regret—sobering him.

Chase was his best friend, but Emmett hadn't told him the truth.

Hell, Emmett had only recently admitted the truth to himself.

He lowered his hand and unwound his fist from Chase's shirt.

"Go on. Finish what you came here to do." He backed away a step so Chase could come for him. It'd be no less than what he deserved. "I realized the truth

I was in denial about the moment I stepped into this house and she wasn't in it."

Chase, chest heaving and unspent anger simmering in his eyes, paused long enough to ask, "What truth was that?"

"I gave up the best thing that ever happened to me. But I did it because I would never make her choose between her family or me. I've never loved someone the way I love her. Like she's my sun. My reason to wake up. Warmth coming at me from all angles. Without her I'm in the shadows and so cold… She loves me, too. She told me and then I had to let her go."

"Tell me it's not because of what I said." Chase's shoulders sagged.

"Don't feel bad about that. Your threat that I'd lose your family—that you'd choose Stefanie—was exactly the reminder I needed. My losing you was what I had to do to make sure *she* didn't lose you."

"Emmett." Chase's expression was chagrined.

He raised an arm, but not to deliver another mind-clattering punch. Chase palmed Emmett's shoulder and squeezed, the move almost…brotherly.

"I was angry when I said that. I would never blacklist you from the family any more than I would Stefanie. You could never do anything that would warrant it." He gestured at Emmett's face, where, no doubt, a bruise was forming. "A black eye, sure, but that's different. You *are* family, Em."

He blinked, taking in what Chase had said and trying to wrap his grieving mind and heartbroken soul around it.

He was family.

"Family doesn't run out on each other," Chase said.

"Mine does." The words were rusty, but no less true.

"Mine *doesn't*. Especially when my sister's heart is on the line. I came here to knock some sense into you. About the resignation from my team, and about the way I know you feel about Stef. Once I stopped seeing red, I realized why you were doing this. You were always loyal to a fault. You're the guy who dives in front of bullets and keeps everyone around him safe. But no one is firing at you, Emmett. You're safe." Chase shrugged like it was a simple realization. Like he hadn't just brought Emmett's world back to center. "You're home."

Since he was a little boy, Emmett had wanted a home. Not only the physical place to lay his head but also a family who would live in service to one another—who would stand by one another no matter the rift. He'd found that in the Fergusons, accepting that if he couldn't have it for himself, at the very least he could be in proximity to it.

"When are you planning on delivering this big speech of love to my sister?" Chase asked.

Then a dash of blond caught the corner of Emmett's eye and he turned to find Stefanie standing in his kitchen, arms folded.

"How about now?"

Miriam stepped in behind her, arms folded as well, her expression speaking for her. *Make it good, buddy.*

"Mimi. Stef." Chase turned, clearly surprised to find his fiancée and his sister here.

A second look at Stefanie told Emmett that his wife was as sad as he felt. Her arms might be crossed, her voice might be strong, but her cheeks and nose were pink, her eyes red and tired like she hadn't slept well outside the circle of his arms.

"What are you two doing here?" Chase asked.

"I suggested we stop by and see how the intervention was going." Miriam snapped her head over to Emmett. "Nice shiner."

"Well?" Stefanie asked, her heat-seeking gaze landing on Emmett. He was aware of Chase and Mimi stepping off to the side.

"How much did you hear?"

"Oh, something about how I was your *sun* and your reason to wake up in the morning."

He swallowed past a thick throat, not sure how she felt about his admission. She'd heard it all.

"We'll be outside." Chase took Miriam's elbow but before they left, he gripped Stef's shoulder. "If you need me—"

"I can handle him."

She wasn't wrong. And now that Emmett had a second chance staring him in the face, he'd be more cooperative. Once Chase and Miriam were gone, Stefanie strolled to the center of the wide kitchen, leaving several feet between them.

"How did you go from wanting nothing from me to feeling everything?"

"Those two can coexist."

"Not in my book."

"I love you so damn much I can hardly breathe without you," he admitted. "But I'd never ask you to choose between me and your family. I'd never ask you to live without them when I knew firsthand how hard that is to do."

"Chase just made it clear there was no escape for you from this family."

"I know."

"I'm not the only one who deserves better. So do you." She took another step in his direction.

The relief he felt when Chase told Emmett he was

home was unparalleled. Like his best friend had voiced what Emmett had been searching for since he was a very small boy. In that same way, Emmett had known what it was like to be half of a whole with Stefanie— to earn her heart and her love when she'd asked for nothing in return.

Emmett was a good husband, and with some work, he knew he could be a great one.

"I'm learning." He swallowed thickly, the faint copper taste of blood on his tongue. "I want it back. Our marriage. Our promise." He lifted her hand, where the wedding band still sat. "Us."

Certainty filled his chest. *This* felt right. Having her here, him admitting that he'd been wrong.

"I want you back. And not just back in my bed. Back in my arms. Back in my life. Next to me every step of the way. I will always protect you, Stef. It's in my nature. It's the way I'm built. But I want to do that because I love you. No other reason."

"I hear you resigned from the protection business," she said, holding his fingers with hers. "What were you planning on doing?"

"I hadn't figured it out yet." A sharp laugh left his chest. "My priority was—always has been—you. I thought it'd be easier if I was out of your life completely. If we didn't accidentally cross paths."

Stef shook her head, tears welling fresh in her eyes.

He swiped them away with his thumb. "Don't cry over me, Stef."

"I'm not." She sniffed. "I'm crying because you're so dumb."

A laugh shook his shoulders. Laughing felt so damn *good* after feeling so damn miserable.

"You were going to leave us behind."

He hadn't thought of it that way.

"Your mom and baby brother left not of their choice. But your dad *chose*. How did it feel to love someone as much as you loved him and not have him around?"

He pushed the truth from his tight throat. "Awful."

"Exactly. *Awful*. You let all of us love you, but you kept your love to yourself."

"I thought... I thought you'd be better off."

She rested her hands on his chest and looked up at him. "Dumb."

He'd missed her warm touch so much that he didn't move a muscle for fear of scaring her off.

"I love you," he said, and it was easy to say to her. Like breathing.

"How much?"

"Enough to marry you. Again."

Her smile broke forth. "We're already married."

"We'll do it better this time. We'll do it right. With your family present. On a beach. In Europe. Whatever you want."

"Whatever, huh?" A mischievous smile curved her lips.

If he had a prayer of getting this woman to forgive him—to make her happy, he'd give her whatever her heart desired. As long as she desired him above all else.

"Whatever," he confirmed, his lips dangerously close to hers. "Can you forgive me?"

She *hmm*ed, but in her shining bright blue eyes, he saw he was already forgiven. It was enough to send his confidence through the roof. His strength returned like Samson with a full head of hair. He was enough for this woman. He was the only man who could fill her heart and make her body sing. She was the only woman for him—the only one who could crack through the wall he'd been trapped behind for years.

"You're for me, honey," he said before he placed a tender kiss on the center of her lips.

"You're for me," she confirmed, gripping his neck tight.

"One favor?" he asked.

"Just one?"

"For now."

"What's that?"

"Don't make me wait until our second wedding night to take you to bed again."

Her warm laugh tickled his lips as he folded her into his arms. "I'd never put myself through that kind of torture *twice*."

She melted into him, her body softening against his as she twined her arms around his neck.

"Is that a yes?" he asked when she gave him a chance to catch his breath.

"Yes."

He bent and scooped her into his arms. "To the wedding or the sex?"

"Yes to both."

He wasted no time carrying her upstairs to his bedroom and showing her exactly how much he missed her. Exactly how much she meant to him and exactly how much he loved her.

On the cusp of her orgasm, he proposed again, vowing to love her forever. On his own release he repeated the word.

Forever.

It sounded like the perfect place to start.

Epilogue

Chase's Dallas mansion had been turned into a virtual winter wonderland. Every room Emmett walked through was draped in silver shimmery something.

Garland.

Ornaments.

Sheer material of some sort hanging on the back wall of the ballroom with curtains of twinkle lights that reminded him of the Sparkle & Shine gala.

He smiled to himself. That was one of his favorite memories.

Two tall Christmas trees stood at either side of a white altar, where their officiant, Reverend James Woods—yes, really—stood with a leather Bible in hand. James was a good friend of the Ferguson family, and Rider and Elle had been overjoyed that Stefanie and Emmett agreed to allow him to perform the ceremony.

Emmett, strangling bow tie be damned, wore a tux.

So did Rider and both of Stefanie's brothers. Chase and Zach were standing to Emmett's left, both groomsmen fighting not to sweat through their black jackets.

Stefanie's dream "Christmas" wedding was happening in Texas in *May*.

When he'd won Stefanie back, Emmett had promised her anything and he'd meant it. She whipped together a plan to renew their vows, employing both Miriam and Penelope to help. After Chase was reelected the mayor of Dallas for another term, Stef pulled the trigger on her own wedding plans.

To get it out of the way so Mimi and Chase can have a wedding, she'd told him.

He loved her giving heart. He loved her passion for other people and her desire to do things big. There were no small celebrations in Stefanie's world, and that Emmett was a part of her world was a gift.

A gift he deserved.

Miriam and Penelope made their ascent up a runner littered with fake snow, both waving at little Olivia, who waved back from her grandmother's lap. Elle smiled and sent Emmett an approving nod. It meant more to him than she could possibly know. He'd tell her later, but for now he simply nodded back.

This was a fairly small affair for the Fergusons; fewer than fifty chairs had butts in them. In one of those chairs sat Emmett's father, who smiled proudly from his seat next to Miriam's mother, Emmett noticed. He suspected his wife was responsible for seating the only two single people in attendance side by side. Another subject to broach later.

His relationship with his father was a work in progress, but when Emmett finally met with him a few months ago, he'd been able to progress past some of the hurt that had haunted them both for years.

The formal music bled into Stefanie's favorite Christmas song: Mariah Carey's "All I Want for Christmas Is You." And then his bride appeared around the corner, arm in arm with her father, her smile as bright and contagious as it had been the day Emmett met her.

Like the first time she strolled to him in a wedding gown, his gut clenched with what he now knew was certainty. That feeling of *rightness*. The expression on his face was no longer the stunned shock of a man who didn't deserve her but the confident acceptance that this woman belonged with him.

She'd told him just last night that she'd decided to legally change her name to Stefanie Keaton. That, and the fact that Chase had claimed Emmett as an honorary brother, was enough to cause Emmett to blink suspiciously scratchy eyes. He'd never accepted the good that'd come his way, but it was hard to resist when it came in tsunami form.

Stefanie stood in front of him now, having been given away by her father, her white dress the same one she'd worn during their original wedding. She claimed it was "lucky."

He couldn't agree more. He was the luckiest man alive.

They joined hands as the reverend began the ceremony. Emmett thumbed the wedding ring that had been at home on her hand for five months. He recalled the story about the widow who wanted the rings to have another life—to be a part of another union that would stand the test of time.

Emmett and Stefanie planned on doing her proud.

"You may kiss your bride," James, the reverend,

said, inspiring quiet chuckles from the crowd when he added, "Again."

Stefanie threw her arms around Emmett's neck and laid one on him. He caught her, lifting her off the floor to hold her close. Applause rippled around them as he lost himself in her mouth.

Never had he imagined he could live a life overflowing with love and happiness, but he'd accepted his fate. And he had this woman in his arms to thank for it.

And thanking her was exactly what he intended to do.

Starting with today, and every day thereafter that he walked this good earth.

* * * * *

COMING NEXT MONTH FROM

HARLEQUIN®

Desire

Available December 31, 2018

Get 4 FREE REWARDS!

We'll send you 2 FREE Books plus 2 FREE Mystery Gifts.

Harlequin® Desire books feature heroes who have it all: wealth, status, incredible good looks... everything but the right woman.

FREE Value Over **$20**

He would never forget the day, ten years ago, when Maya
Richardson had walked through his door looking for a
job. She'd been a godsend, helping Ayden grow Stewart
Investments into the company it was today. Thinking
of her brought a smile to Ayden's face. How could it
not? Not only was she the best assistant he'd ever had,
Maya had fascinated him. Utterly and completely. Maya
had hidden an exceptional figure beneath professional
clothing and kept her hair in a tight bun. But Ayden had
often wondered what it would be like to throw her over
his desk and muss her up. Five years ago, he hadn't gone
quite that far, but he had crossed a boundary.

Maya had been devastated over her breakup with her
boyfriend. She'd come to him for comfort, and, instead,
Ayden had made love to her. Years of wondering what
it would be like to be with Maya had erupted into a

passionate encounter. Their one night together had been so explosive that the next morning Ayden had needed to take a step back to regain his perspective. He'd had to put up his guard; otherwise, he would have hurt her badly. He thought he'd been doing the right thing, but Maya hadn't thought so. In retrospect, Ayden wished he'd never given in to temptation. But he had, and he'd lost a damn good assistant. Maya had quit, and Ayden hadn't seen or heard from her since.

Shaking his head, Ayden strode to his desk and picked up the phone, dialing the recruiter who'd helped him find Carolyn. He wasn't looking forward to this process. It had taken a long time to find and train Carolyn. Before her, Ayden had dealt with several candidates walking into his office thinking they could ensnare him.

No, he had someone else in mind. A hardworking, dedicated professional who could read his mind without him saying a word and who knew how to handle a situation in his absence. Someone who knew about the big client he'd always wanted to capture but never could attain. She also had a penchant for numbers and research like no one he'd ever seen, not even Carolyn.

Ayden knew exactly who he wanted. He just needed to find out where she'd escaped to.

Don't miss what happens next!
At the CEO's Pleasure by Yahrah St. John,
part of her Stewart Heirs series!

Available January 2019 wherever
Harlequin® Desire books and ebooks are sold.

www.Harlequin.com

Love Harlequin romance?

DISCOVER.

Be the first to find out about promotions,
news and exclusive content!

Facebook.com/HarlequinBooks

Twitter.com/HarlequinBooks

Instagram.com/HarlequinBooks

Pinterest.com/HarlequinBooks

ReaderService.com

EXPLORE.

Sign up for the Harlequin e-newsletter and
download a free book from any series at
TryHarlequin.com.

CONNECT.

Join our Harlequin community to share
your thoughts and connect with other
romance readers!
Facebook.com/groups/HarlequinConnection

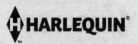

THE WORLD IS BETTER WITH

Romance

Harlequin has everything from contemporary, passionate and heartwarming to suspenseful and inspirational stories.

Whatever your mood, we have a romance just for you!

Connect with us to find your next great read, special offers and more.

f /HarlequinBooks

🐦 @HarlequinBooks

www.HarlequinBlog.com

www.Harlequin.com/Newsletters

♦ HARLEQUIN®

A *Romance* FOR EVERY MOOD™

www.Harlequin.com